TURLU

LEO PERUTZ (1882–1957) was

to Vienna, where he settled until the Nazi Anschluss drove him out in 1938 and he emigrated to Israel. He was employed as an actuary with an insurance company until he turned to writing. His first novel (*The Third Bullet*) was written in 1915 while he was recovering from a war-wound. Perutz is now considered one of the finest historical novelists of our age – for Graham Greene he was "a craftsman of the first order".

JOHN BROWNJOHN, one of Britain's foremost translators from the German, has translated several of Perutz's novels for Harvill, including *The Swedish Cavalier*, which won the Schlegel-Tieck translation prize.

Also by Leo Perutz in English translation

LEONARDO'S JUDAS

THE MARQUIS OF BOLIBAR

BY NIGHT UNDER THE STONE BRIDGE

SAINT PETER'S SNOW

LITTLE APPLE

THE SWEDISH CAVALIER

THE MASTER OF THE DAY OF JUDGMENT

Leo Perutz

TURLUPIN

Translated from the German
by John Brownjohn

THE HARVILL PRESS
LONDON

First published in Austria in 1924 with the title *Turlupin*
Reissued by Paul Zsolnay Verlag, Vienna, in 1984

First published in Great Britain in 1996
by The Harvill Press,
84 Thornhill Road,
London N1 1RD

First impression

A CIP catalogue record for this book is
available from the British Library.

ISBN 1 86046 178 6

Designed and typeset in Bell at
Libanus Press, Marlborough, Wiltshire

Printed and bound by Butler & Tanner
at Selwood Printing, Burgess Hill

Turlupin

[1]

THE RECORD OF the trial of Michel Babaut, a former justices' clerk arraigned before the Royal Appellate Court in Paris on charges of atheism, perjury, and sundry acts of violence, a lengthy hearing which ended in November 1642, alludes to a most peculiar incident. On being informed that the court had sentenced him to eleven years in the galleys and a fine of six hundred livres, the condemned man roared with laughter, turned to his judges, and – so the record states – scornfully remarked that it was a good long way to Marseille, and that he intended, with their lordships' permission, to take part in "the grand shuttlecock tournament" to which Monsieur de Saint-Chéron had invited all his friends.

The court record does not indicate how the judges, assessors and clerks received this remark. Although they may simply have shaken their heads in bewilderment, it is fair to assume that most of those present were thoroughly alive to the menace inherent in the condemned man's words. Paris was teeming with nebulous rumours at this period. Dark tidings of great events in store were relayed from house to house and mouth to mouth. The grand shuttlecock tournament . . . This cryptic phrase recurred again and again, and each sought to interpret it in his own way. None knew precisely what was in the offing, but all seemed cognizant of when it would happen. A lampoon on the Duc de Guise, couched in clumsy doggerel and signed "Etienne, who tells all", went the rounds early in November. It opened with the words "Hither, Duc de Guise, you must! You, too, are doomed to bite the dust!" and named St Martin's Day, or November 11th, as the day of the shuttlecock tournament ("Good people of Paris, pray mark what I say: the feathers will fly on St Martin's Day!") In so doing, it clearly told the Parisians no more than they already knew. Two weeks earlier, a certain Pierre Lamin, whose job it was to collect arrears of hearth-money for his employer, a tax farmer's sublessee, stated in his report (*Archives nationaux, E XIX a 134*) that people in various parts of the city had told him, "one and all, as if by prior arrangement", that they had no money in the house, but that at Martinmas – of that he could rest assured – they would call on his master in person and settle accounts with him in full.

Written twenty years later, Madame d'Ouchy's recollections of the time of Richelieu and the Regency (*Mémoires de Mme d'Ouchy, d'après ses papiers personnels*, A. Delion-Drouet, Grenoble, 1892), contain the following passage: "During the night of 10th–11th November [1642] there appeared at our house a man who had five years earlier spent some weeks in our employ as a footman. With tears in his eyes, he demanded to speak with Monsieur le Maréchal [Mme d'Ouchy's father] and was conducted to the first floor. A quarter of an hour later my father came to my room, pale with agitation, and bade me make ready for the road. It was two o'clock in the morning when we left the city, bound for M. le Comte de Bouillon's estate at Sedan. I had not had time to provide myself with even the barest necessities. We reached Epernay." And, some pages below: "This journey had cost my father 1200 gold livres and two of our best carriage horses."

They never got to Sedan. M. le Maréchal returned to Paris only two days later, Martinmas having passed without incident. The *Gazette de la cour* (14th November, 1642) stated that a riotous mob had assembled near the Hôtel Lavan, and that the Duc de Noirmoutier and a count belonging to the Mömpelgard family had duelled with sword and pistol in the pinewood at Vincennes, watched by a sizeable throng of interested spectators. Another newspaper, the *Gazette de France* (16th November, 1642), reported that a pastrycook's seven-year-old daughter had, on 11th November, been abducted from the Convent of the Feuillants by two masked gallants, and that on the afternoon of the same day a councillor for petitions had been dragged from his carriage and manhandled by the mob. These, however, were incidents of minor importance, and were deemed quite commonplace in the Paris of Richelieu and Louis XIII. As for the event that had been presaged for so many weeks and veiled in the words "the grand shuttlecock tournament", all Paris and all France had awaited it in vain.

For all that, St Martin's Day 1642 by no means faded from the public mind. Throughout the popular literature of the seventeenth century – street songs, triolets, printed pamphlets, fairground ballads, poems extemporized by strolling players – allusions to that Martinmas recur again and again, initially in language expressive of bitter disappointment, later in a tone of sorrowful resignation. "St Martin's Day" did not acquire an ironical and jocular flavour until the beginning of the eighteenth century, when it became roughly synonymous with "the Greek Calends". It last appeared in the writings of Denis Diderot. When Diderot, aged twenty-five, learned the details of the barbaric execution of the murderer Saulnier, he noted in his journal:

"Not a word, not a syllable shall pass my lips! What can I do but wait and hope for a new St Martin's Day, which must sooner or later dawn and will change the world entirely" (*Mémoires, correspondance et ouvrages inédits*, Paris, 1830).

If Diderot, who dreamed of a bloodless new order, a spiritual revolution, had guessed the terrible secret latent in the expression "St Martin's Day", he would never have penned those words.

Documents shrouded in two centuries of archival gloom have since come to light. We now know that a St Bartholomew's Day massacre of the French nobility had been planned for Martinmas 1642. Seventeen thousand people – all in France who bore a noble name – were to be slaughtered in the course of that one day. Such was the grand shuttlecock tournament during which the heads of the Rohans, the Guises, the Épernons, the Montbazons, the Luynes, the Nevers, the Choiseuls, the de Crécys, the Bellegardes, the La Forces, and the Angoulêmes were to go flying through the air like shuttlecocks.

Who was the author of this frightful plan? Who had devised it? Whose hand wove the threads together? No need here to refer to the findings of d'Avenels, R. Perkins, or D. Rocas. In France in the year 1642, there was only one man in whose head this grand and terrible design could have originated: Armand-Jean du Plessis, Cardinal Duc de Richelieu.

Let us briefly pause to examine the man, his work, and his age.

Though less than fifty-seven years old at this time, the Duc de Richelieu was an ailing man already overcast by the shadow of death, which would claim him only a few weeks later. His lifelong ambition had been to destroy the power of the French establishment and wrest political authority from the hands of the nobility. For this one objective's sake he had incurred the hatred of the entire world. His dream was the greatness of France, his weapons were dissimulation and guile, brutality and ferocity. And now, on the threshold of death, he saw his life's work in jeopardy: a docile weakling on the throne of France; at the king's side a woman whom countless humiliations had transformed into his, Richelieu's, bitter enemy; and, on the national borders, in Flanders, Lorraine and Spain, his old adversaries, Marie de Rohan, the Ducs d'Epernon and de Vendôme, the Comte de Beaupuis, Maréchal d'Estrées. All were counting the days, and all thought their time had come. They had almost written him off.

Richelieu's terrible scheme may have occurred to him at a moment when, in the depths of depression and despair, his indomitable will rebelled against his ravaged body. His last and most terrible coup would be directed against all who stood between him and his goal, and they included the king himself. A new idea had taken shape in Cromwell's England: at the end of his life, Richelieu envisioned the creation of a French republic.

The letters and memoirs of those close to him contain numerous references to the unmentionable thing that preyed on their minds.

"I know whereon his plans were founded. I was acquainted with his resources, his confederates, his ultimate intentions, but these are matters best forgotten, not committed to paper." (Letter from the Comte de Brienne to the French ambassador in Rome. *Brienne, Louis-Henri de Loménie, Comte de, Secrétaire d'Etat,* D. Monnier, Paris, 1887.)

"Do not ask me! It would mean revealing to men that which I would fain conceal from God Himself." (Comte de Chavigny to the Duc d'Enghien. R. Marieul: *Histoire des princes de Condé,* Paris, 1854.)

"I knew all but had perforce to keep silent, for his vengeance would have been terrible." (Pierre Séguier: *Mémoires,* Coll. Le Tellier, Geneva, 1904.)

"I was standing in the antechamber with M. de Motteville when I saw M. Guitard, the captain of the Scottish Guard, emerge from the salon. 'I have been commanded,' he said, 'not to intervene if a riot breaks out in the streets tomorrow. Very well, but I shall request a copy of that order in writing.' I looked at M. de Motteville, but he affected to have heard nothing." (Navailles, R., Duc de: *Mémoires,* Paris, 1842.)

Trembling and bowed down beneath their burden of responsibility, Richelieu's handful of initiates stood by him, as incapable of grasping the dimensions of his idea as they were of opposing him.

And Richelieu himself?

The bible he used during his latter years bears an inscription in his own handwriting:"I can see no way but this. Whether good come of it or ill, I desire my share of both."

Those words are to be found in the margin of *Judges* xx, which recounts the annihilation of the tribe of Benjamin.

Was Richelieu's plan impracticable? Absurd? Insane? A historical anachronism?

It is one of human history's great enigmas that the French Revolution did not break out until 1789.

France was already ripe for it in 1642. Present in that year was the very same combination of people, ideas and special circumstances that conduced to the fall of the monarchy at the end of the eighteenth century.

As in Richelieu's day, the population had been impoverished by a long and costly war and driven to despair by an unfairly distributed burden of taxation. As in Richelieu's day, the throne of France was occupied by a Habsburg, Anne of Austria, who had remained alien to her people. She, too, had a Comte de Fersen in the person of Buckingham. And, where Washington's War of Independence set the pattern for revolution in 1779, the young people of France looked in 1642 to Cromwell's struggle against the Stuart king.

The great protagonists of 1789, too, were ready to hand a hundred and fifty years earlier. Bailly? We find his counterpart in Omer Talon, the attorney-general whose speech to the Parliament of Paris "moved the populace to tears and vexed the king's ministers". Lafayette? In the middle of the seventeenth century, the name of that handsome, ambitious, popularity-seeking general was Louis II, Prince de Condé. The Girondists?

We encounter them in the spiritual movement that culminated, under Mazarin's premiership, in the Fronde. Philippe Egalité? Gaston d'Orléans, Louis XIII's contemptible and unkingly brother, would undoubtedly have defected to the people at the first shot. General Hoche? The Comte de Turenne would have defended the revolutionary cause against all external enemies. Talleyrand? His role would have been played to perfection by Cardinal de Retz.

And Mirabeau? Who was the Mirabeau of 1642?

The Mirabeau of 1642 was the Vicomte de Saint-Chéron.

Saint-Chéron belonged to an old noble family from the Dauphiné. Though destined in his youth for the priesthood, he quit holy orders early on. When, at the age of twenty-seven, he proposed to wed the daughter of a Blois tavern-keeper, his father prevented the marriage by obtaining a warrant from the king under which young Saint-Chéron was arrested in the tavern one night and subsequently imprisoned. His father died within months, and his case lapsed into oblivion. By the time he left Vincennes Prison seventeen years later, he was a prematurely aged man and a mortal foe of king and aristocracy.

To earn a living, he assumed the name "Monsieur Gaspard" and took employment as a clothier's assistant in the Saint-Thomas quarter of the Louvre. In the evenings, when his master's shop was shut, he would betake himself to the Place de Grève, the old ramparts, the timber yards beside the Seine, or the wine shops of Suresne and Saint-Antoine, and preach rebellion against the affluent, against idlers lolling in coaches and carriages, against tax farmers and their mistresses, against venal judges, against royal favourites greedy for pensions and benefices, against plumed hats and peruques, against the whole crumbling edifice of state. On 4th October 1642, having stationed himself on the steps of the church of Saint-Jacques de la Bougerie and publicly branded the king "a crowned monkey", he was arrested by a lieutenant of the royal bodyguard. Some Seine bargemen, who were friends of his, rescued him just as he was being marched off to the Châtelet. Two days later he was sent for by the Duc de Richelieu.

The interview took place at the Palais Cardinal, in the secluded drawing-room where envoys from the exiled Mazarin would ten years later be received in audience by the queen. It lasted nearly two hours. When it was over, the cardinal conducted his visitor through empty rooms and along dark passages to a side door that opened on to the banks of the Seine.

In the days immediately thereafter, preliminary references to the shuttlecock tournament at Martinmas were heard in the streets of Paris. On 11th November, St Martin's Day, the Vicomte de Saint-Chéron was to lead a mob against the Hôtel Lavan, where the cardinal's enemies customarily gathered to confer in secret. The storming and burning of the Hôtel Lavan would be the signal for a massacre of the nobility throughout France and the overthrow of the monarchy.

The statesman had allied himself with the rebel to give France a republic.

But it was not to be. Fate went its own way. Old, moribund France would once more triumph over the ideas of a modern age. The world was not to be denied the splendour of the Sun King's reign.

In order to thwart the plans of Richelieu, the titan, destiny made use of a simpleton named Turlupin.

[2]

IN THE RUE des Douze Apôtres, not far from the cutlers' hall and the cattle market, stood a small barbershop belonging to a widow named Jacqueline Sabot. Although her husband had been a skilled practitioner, he died leaving her nothing but the tools of his trade, a list of taverns where a pitcher of wine could be had for as little as two sous, and the responsibility for his requiem Masses. At first, having in her youth been a kitchen maid in the house of M. des Yvetaux, she endeavoured to earn a living for herself and her child by making cream tartlets, little honey cakes and Florentines, and hawking them through the streets. This trade earned her little, however, and, since the chandlers, clothiers, cutlers and twine-makers of the neighbourhood made a habit of repairing to the Rue des Douze Apôtres at midday to exchange gossip and have their chins shaved, she had given house-room to a youth adept at wielding the dead man's scissors, plasters, towels, unguent jars, and pomade pots.

This youth, Tancrède Turlupin by name, was a foundling. As a child of two he had been discovered on the steps of the Trinitarian church one cold winter's morning and adopted some days later by an elderly basket-weaver named Daniel Turlupin. When his foster-father perished in the great fire that destroyed the Saint-Antoine quarter in 1632, the boy scraped a living for a while by selling pins, hair clasps and belt buckles at weekly markets. At sixteen, thanks to some kindly benefactors, he was schooled in the wig-maker's and barber's trade.

Tancrède Turlupin was a dreamer, and full of odd whims. He not only defied contemporary custom by disdaining to wear a wig but walked the streets hatless. Despite his youth he had a lock of white hair which he allowed to fall across his brow where all could see it, for this was the peculiarity that would some day, or so he hoped, enable his unknown father to recognize him.

He devoted much thought to his father's identity and rank, though he never mentioned the subject and went about his work in self-absorbed silence. He was far from handsome, being an exceptionally tall young man with a bony face, thick lips and crooked teeth, but the widow took a fancy to him notwithstanding, and his kindness to her daughter, little Nicole, thoroughly endeared him to her. She had grown weary of her widowhood. When Tancrède Turlupin had been lodging with her for a year, she ceded her late husband's bed to him and spent her nights on the bench beside the stove. She also had their portraits painted on a medallion – mistress and journeyman encircled by garlands of roses – and presented it to him on his name-day, together with an intimation that he should treasure the said medallion and wear it on a chain around his neck.

This he did, but only to oblige her, for he had no real intention of ending his days as a barber in the Rue des Douze Apôtres. Having been rescued from a burning house at the age of eleven, he had ever thereafter felt a private certainty that he was destined for great things – that fate had preserved his life for a purpose. He waited patiently in the expectation that his hour was bound to strike. While applying himself to his work with razor in one hand and towel in the other, he dreamed of his future. He saw himself in helmet and cuirass, a king's officer leading his cavalrymen and halberdiers into a Spanish town that had just surrendered to him. He saw himself as a nobleman traversing the countryside in a well-upholstered carriage, with local magistrates hurrying up to pay their respects and bringing gifts of flowers and fruit and cakes to the carriage door. He saw himself as a parliamentarian in a long robe, a canon of Nôtre Dame, an ambassador at foreign courts, an attorney general, a viceroy. And, while daydreaming, he found that his work proceeded of its own accord.

In the evening, when it grew dark, he would sit beside the stove and, while the widow chopped greens and swedes into the soup, peruse a book entitled *The Seal of Wisdom*, which had been written by Maria, the sister of Mosis, a very learned Jewess. He read it through again and again from beginning to end, profoundly affected by its disclosure of the world's marvels and mysteries. He knew, because this book had taught him, that his destiny did not lie in his hands alone. There were good and evil powers, so it was necessary to secure God's aid. In order to win God over, Tancrède Turlupin observed the fasts and all the other precepts of the Church. He also performed acts of charity, and never passed a beggar without giving alms. This he did for prudence and safety's sake, because he secretly detested beggars. He not only wished them more misfortune than had ever afflicted a living soul but would gladly have strangled them all with both hands. They were God's spies, impostors, miserable traitors. They collected alms as though levying a tribute. They promptly cursed anyone who passed them by unheeding, and their words ascended heavenwards until they gained God's ear. They were conscious of their power and ever eager to despoil honest, hard-working folk. Tancrède Turlupin ground his teeth with suppressed fury when giving them his small change.

Such was the dreamer and simpleton who made his way across the timber-built Pont-Rouge at noon on 8th November 1642, carrying some freshly-honed razors and a cabbage purchased at the vegetable market.

[3]

He had just come from the knife-grinder's and was in an ill humour because of the aforesaid beggars, of whom he had already passed fourteen that day. Cripples, old men, women suckling babies – all had lined his route and demanded alms as though in league against him. Having already doled out every copper he possessed, he had nothing left in his pocket but a newly-minted silver eight-sou piece, and that he begrudged them.

It was raining. It had rained all morning, and the sky was veiled in cloud. The wind was stripping the last withered leaves from the branches of the maple and acacia trees that peeped over the garden walls and wrought-iron gates on the other side of the Seine. Tancrède Turlupin was cold and soaked to the skin. He strode along briskly, eager to get back to the barbershop and warm himself at the stove, but no sooner had he started across the bridge than he sighted yet another beggar, a man with a wooden leg and a matted red beard. He was seated with his back against the balustrade, right beside the steps that led down to the island. His legs were fully extended so that everyone had to step over him willy-nilly. There was no avoiding him, the bridge was too narrow.

Turlupin paused, and a stream of irate, resentful thoughts surged through him.

"There's another, the fifteenth this accursed day! They're out to get me – they won't rest content till they've extracted the last sou from my pocket. I know this one, he also goes begging around the cobblers' shops in the Rue du Chapitre. He ought to be ashamed of himself, he's not even old and he's healthy into the bargain. Chopping wood – two arms are all you need for chopping wood, but no, he prefers to sit there and pocket honest folk's money. An eight-sou piece would suit him very nicely. In two years he'd have enough to employ footmen and keep a carriage. As for me, I toil away from dawn to dusk. It's unjust!"

Perplexed and irresolute, Turlupin watched a barge laden with empty wine casks gliding slowly down the Seine past the flour mills. Turn back? No, he had no wish to do that either. Another beggar would be sure to be lying in wait for him on the next bridge. He took the eight-sou piece from his pocket and walked on with it clutched in his hand.

On drawing nearer, however, Turlupin saw that the beggar was sitting there with his eyes shut. He seemed to be asleep, but even asleep he continued to demand alms by holding out his cap. It occurred to Turlupin that he might cheat the beggar and keep his money by sneaking past him unseen. The idea appealed to him. He tiptoed past, noiseless as a rat, then broke into a run. He ran till he was out of breath, and it was only when he reached the opposite bank that he paused to glance timidly back.

The beggar was asleep no longer. He had scrambled up and was leaning on his crutch in the middle of the bridge, gazing at the fugitive.

Turlupin was startled and disappointed. "Go to hell, you rogue, and find someone there who'll give you an eight-sou piece!" he hissed, and angrily continued on his way. "That was no beggar, that was a fraud, a good-for-nothing, a buffoon. He deserves no charity. Feigning sleep and hoodwinking people! Did he think I'd be deceived?"

Annoyed with himself, he angrily shook his head, brushed his misgivings aside, and resolved to forget the whole affair as quickly as possible. But the farther he got from the bridge, the heavier his heart became. He had kept his eight sous, yes, but he had thereby forfeited the divine assistance he needed so badly. God would be angry with him and withhold his aid. Worst of all, the many hundreds of sous he had previously distributed in alms had been expended to no avail and were as good as wasted. His recent action now struck him as a great and unpardonable act of folly. He was already in the Rue des Apôtres when he decided to return to the bridge and placate the Almighty.

But it was as if all the evil powers had combined to keep a repentant sinner at odds with his Maker. The alleyways through which he had to pass were suddenly filled with hustle and bustle. It being noon and the rain having ceased, clerks poured out of their offices by the hundred, noblemen galloped through the streets with their retainers, students linked arms and barred Turlupin's path, sedan chairs and carriages, heavy-laden mules and ponderous vegetable carts compelled him to hug the walls and wait. Almost an hour elapsed before he finally regained the banks of the Seine.

It was then demonstrated to him, not for the first time, that Satan is adept at using even sacred rites for his own ends. A sizeable procession was wending its way along the river bank, and walking at its head beneath a baldaquin, surrounded by his priests, was the archbishop's coadjutor in full clerical garb. Turlupin had to stop and wait once more. At last the way was clear. He reached for his eight-sou piece, but was surprised to find the beggar gone from the bridge.

At the spot where the man with the wooden leg and the red beard had been sitting, a municipal guardsman now stood looking over the balustrade at the brushwood and gravel paths on the island below. Not far away, frowning with annoyance, a nobleman lounged beside his horse while a liveried servant knelt on the ground before him and scraped the mire of the streets from his top-boots.

Turlupin went up to the guardsman and inquired the beggar's whereabouts. Turning, the man looked first at Turlupin and then his cabbage. Then, without a word, he pointed downwards. There, at the foot of the steps that linked the island with the bridge, lay the beggar. An old woman was cradling his head in her lap. His ragged coat was bloodstained, and there was a cloth over his face. The nobleman's horse had knocked him down and kicked him to death.

At first, Turlupin experienced a kind of relief at the way things had turned out. He had done his utmost to propitiate the Almighty. His intentions had been of the best, and the eight sous were now his to keep. Quite suddenly, however, he was assailed by a thought that filled him with dread: the beggar with the wooden leg and red beard might even now be standing before God's throne, but he was not accusing his murderer; all the man's wrath was directed at him, Tancrède Turlupin. "And today, little more than an hour ago," he could hear him saying, "someone passed by without giving me alms. Not the smallest coin did he give me – indeed, he derided me." – "Describe him to me!" cried the Almighty, his face darkening. "Describe him to me, that I may recognize him!" – "He wore patched shoes and a blue coat," the beggar pursued. – "Go on!" cried the Almighty. "Many a man in Paris wears a blue coat and patched shoes." – "He was holding a cabbage in his hand, the kind you can buy for two sous at a vegetable market." – "Go on!" the Almighty boomed from his throne. "Is that all you can tell me?" – "Bushy eyebrows. He was still young, but he had a lock of white hair falling across his brow." – "A lock of white hair?" exclaimed the Almighty. "Then it was Tancrède Turlupin. Enough said, you may go. Tancrède Turlupin! Very well, I'll make a note of his name. So he withholds alms from the poor!"

Turlupin gave a start. He looked around distractedly, and, as if it would dispel the thoughts that were tormenting him, brushed the lock of white hair off his forehead.

At that moment the nobleman remounted his horse. Before riding on, however, he beckoned to the manservant.

"Renauld," he said, "I forgot to ask your master the time of the funeral."

"Excellency," replied the manservant, "the mourners are to assemble in the Église des Trinitaires at two o'clock tomorrow."

To Tancrède Turlupin, who overheard them, these words seemed a divine commandment. The Église des Trinitaires at two o'clock . . . His first afternoon customers appeared in the barbershop at that hour, granted, but they could wait. He was determined to join the beggar's funeral cortège and purchase a candle for the altar.

Meanwhile, the widow was impatiently awaiting Turlupin's return. Unable to account for his protracted absence, she kept emerging from her kitchen and stepping outside the shop to look for him. Toward one o'clock there appeared, not Turlupin, but Daniel Coquereau, a worthy, respectable citizen who had for many years kept a grocer's shop on the corner of the Rue St Jacques. He came several times a week to pay his respects to Madame Sabot, having taken a fancy to the young and still quite pretty widow. He kept no kitchen and disliked eating-houses, so he made a habit of turning up at meal times.

The widow greeted him with the courtesy due to a man whose position seemed secure in every respect.

"Monsieur Coquereau," she said, "I'm delighted to see you. We'll eat together, if it suits you."

"Madame Sabot, I am, as you know, your obedient servant," Monsieur Coquereau replied, judicially inhaling the aroma of cooking, "but you do me more honour than I deserve."

"It would give me pleasure," said the widow, and proceeded to lay the table.

Monsieur Coquereau caught sight of little Nicole, who ran out of the kitchen and into the parlour in pursuit of the cat.

"Why, there you are, Nicole!" he exclaimed. "Wait, let me look at you. I've a pretty blue hair ribbon for you at home. You're getting bigger every day."

"She takes after her father in every way," said the widow. She deposited the soup tureen on the table, together with a covered casserole, the bread basket, the salt cellar, and a pitcher of wine. "Be seated, Monsieur Coquereau, and help yourself. Those are morels," she added, indicating the casserole. "I like to eat them hot, straight from the saucepan. Nicole, leave the cat in peace and come to table!"

Monsieur Coquereau had brought his knife and spoon with him. "Morels make an excellent dish," he observed. "One has to know how to prepare them, that's all."

"They're the finest dish in the world," the widow declared, "provided one covers them well and simmers them on the stove with some parsley and a little pepper. November, that's the season for them."

"Parsley makes any dish tastier," remarked Monsieur Coquereau, knotting a napkin around his neck.

"You're much mistaken, Monsieur Coquereau," said the widow, kindly but with dignity. "Parsley is quite unsuited to certain dishes. Monsieur des Yvetaux was a sensible man in other respects, but I recall an occasion when he asked me to cook him a carp with parsley. I failed to understand, even then, how a man of taste could make such an error of judgement."

"Carp with parsley?" cried Monsieur Coquereau, almost choking on a mouthful. "I don't believe it! Carp with parsley? Upon my soul, nothing could be more absurd."

At that moment Turlupin appeared in the doorway. He mumbled a greeting, removed his coat, and added the freshly-sharpened razors to the rest. Then he went over to the table and asked Madame Sabot's permission, being as cold as he was, to eat his soup beside the kitchen stove.

"And then," he went on, "tomorrow at two o'clock – it's only on account of a funeral. There's a possibility that Monsieur Pigeot – you know, the dyer – he may turn up at two, for his wig, but he won't mind waiting and I'll be back by three. I think it'll be a very short service – no ceremonial or speechifying."

"A funeral, eh?" said the widow, puzzled because she knew that Turlupin had no friends or relations. "Who's to be buried?"

"A dead man, who else?" Turlupin replied, looking glum and ill at ease. "Someone who died today."

"Aha!" Monsieur Coquereau exclaimed jocularly. "It's dark at night, and a man can ride faster than he can walk. Six mules and six hedgehogs make a dozen, and most folk's noses are in the middle of their faces. Did you hear that, Madame Sabot? They're going to bury a dead man tomorrow."

The widow, who knew her Turlupin, realized that she would get nothing more out of the taciturn and uncommunicative young man, so she changed the subject.

"One hears every day of people dying quite suddenly overnight," she said. "The wet weather's to blame – all this rain and cold wind. One has to take great care. It's best not to venture outdoors at all. Our good king is ill, too. I know that for a fact, because a procession passed through the streets today to pray for his recovery at the Dominicans'. May God grant him his holy protection."

Monsieur Coquereau beckoned her closer and, indicating Turlupin with the tip of his knife, whispered confidentially in her ear.

"He's deceiving you, it's as plain as a pikestaff. He has an assignation with some girl at two o'clock tomorrow, but who cares? You surely can't take any pleasure in the love of that oaf."

[4]

NEXT DAY, ATTIRED in the grey taffeta suit which he customarily reserved for feast days, Turlupin set off with a two-pound red wax candle under his arm. The gloomy autumn day was chill and damp, the sky swathed in dark, threatening clouds. Turlupin walked fast, eager to reach the church before rain spoiled his new coat.

But when he turned into the narrow street that led from the Place de la Trinité, past the great grain scales, to the Trinitarian Convent, he found it obstructed by a whole array of cabriolets, carriages and saddle-horses, all of which appeared to be waiting there, and among them, chatting together in groups of three or four, stood the coachmen, grooms and lackeys.

"Damnation!" Turlupin muttered. "It must be a nobleman's wedding or a christening – I've no hope of getting through. Or are all these carriages here because *The Tragedy of Abel's Death* is playing at the Hôtel Bourgogne? Whatever the reason, those dogs of lackeys would hurl me into the gutter – they'd do so for sport and spend an hour laughing at it. Either that, or one of those horses would lash out and kick me in the chest like that beggar yesterday. I rue the day and the hour when I crossed his path."

He stood there, sullenly eyeing the painted coat of arms on a carriage door, a mailed fist surmounted by a fess and two golden thistles. Then he turned and retraced his steps to the Place de la Trinité in search of another route.

He made his way along the Rue de Fer and the Rue St Nicolas, but when at last he reached the convent square he was balked once more. Thousands upon thousands of people were standing tightly packed together, shoulder to shoulder, as if the entire city had arranged to meet outside the Trinitarian Convent. "Devil take these gawkers and idlers!" snarled Turlupin. "Do they have to be here, even for the funeral of a wretched beggar?" And he pushed and shoved his way forwards, because the tower clock was striking two, and he realized that he would be too late unless he succeeded in forging a path through the crowd.

"Hey!" exclaimed one of the people whom he was kicking and elbowing aside. "I've been here two hours – I had to fight for this place. We all hope to see something, so kindly grant me my due."

It was Monsieur Chevrette, the jobbing tailor from the Rue des Apôtres. He turned to look at his tormentor.

"Why, if it isn't Monsieur Turlupin ," he said. "So you're the one that's been flattening his nose against my back!"

"Monsieur Chevrette!" Turlupin exclaimed in surprise. "Are you also here for the funeral?"

"Why else?" the tailor retorted. "But it's ceased to be a pleasure. Too many people."

He produced a piece of fried fish from his pocket and began to eat it.

"Fried fish," he said. "My breakfast, today being a maigre day."

"So you're here too," said Turlupin, still puzzled. "Did you know him?"

"Did I know him? Strange question! How should I have known him? And you, Monsieur Turlupin? Don't tell me he visited your barbershop every day!"

"That would have been the last straw," Turlupin growled, bristling at the very thought. "I'd have shown him the door in short order."

"They say the funeral oration will be delivered by Monsieur de Paris, His Grace the Archbishop in person," said the tailor.

"The Archbishop in person?" cried Turlupin. "By God, that's no small honour for a man who did nothing but thrust his wooden leg at all and sundry."

"I don't know if he had a wooden leg," said the tailor, "but it's quite possible, given that he fought for Mother Church at La Rochelle."

"Perhaps, but that must have been a long time ago," said Turlupin. "He was a pitiable sight the last time I saw him."

And he had a mental picture of the beggar seated on the bridge near the steps in his tattered coat, waiting, cap in hand, for alms.

"His son," interposed a short, fat, asthmatic fellow, " – they say his son received the news while breakfasting with Mademoiselle de Saint-Luc at the Jardin Vignerol."

"Mademoiselle de Saint-Luc?" said the tailor. "Who's she?"

"A dancer," the fat man wheezed, "a young prostitute. In a word, a promiscuous flibbertigibbet. As soon as he heard the news he sent the musicians home and summoned his carriage."

"Well, I'll be damned," muttered Turlupin, "so his son keeps a carriage. He has the gall to keep a carriage while the likes of us have to pay for it all – the breakfast, the musicians, the carriage, and Mademoiselle de Saint-Luc."

He sighed, overcome with rancour and regret at the thought of life's injustices.

"There are too many of them," he said. "They're a regular pest. They squander our money and make paupers of us."

The words were repeated in a gruff voice. "They squander our money and make paupers of us," said a big, corpulent man standing close beside Turlupin. "You never spoke a truer word, sir. Remember that some day, when Monsieur de Saint-Chéron calls you out into the streets."

"Monsieur de Saint-Chéron?" said Turlupin. "One is for ever hearing his name, but I'm not acquainted with the gentleman."

"Make way for Monsieur le Duc d'Enghien!" called a voice, and all at once the crowd began to shove and jostle. Oaths rent the air, someone cried out that his hat had fallen off, and Turlupin found himself suddenly propelled toward the middle of the square.

"The Duc d'Enghien, that's the son of Monsieur le Prince," said the tailor, who was still at Turlupin's side. "They say that he and Monsieur intend to meet in the church today, after an estrangement lasting three years."

"God forbid!" came a voice from the crowd. "Let them remain estranged, it's better so. If they make it up, those two, the first thing they'll do is contrive another war – on the Rhine, in Spain or Brabant. It's a certainty."

"Oho!" exclaimed the tailor. "Not so fast, not so fast! I reckon Monsieur le Cardinal would have something to say about that."

Just then a passage opened up, and through the silent throng strode a tall, slim man in top-boots and a flame-red coat. Escorted by a retinue of noblemen and officers, he made for the church door.

"That's Monsieur le Duc d'Enghien," hissed the tailor, and swept off his hat, but Turlupin was no longer looking at him. In obedience to a sudden impulse, he had detached himself from the crowd and was following the duke like one of the noblemen in his train.

Once inside the vestibule he came to a halt. The funeral service had already begun. The priest's *Domine exaudi* rang out from the altar, and the choir responded with *Fiant aures tuae intendentes.*

Turlupin proceeded no further. Sitting huddled on the flagstones just in front of him was an old beggar woman. To propitiate the Almighty, he tossed her his silver eight-sou piece.

"There," he told her, feeling thoroughly pleased with himself, "that's a handsome gift, but take care no one steals it from you. I'll wager you don't receive such charity every day."

The crone made no response. The coin was lying in her lap, but her milky eyes failed to see it. Her toothless mouth shaped the words of a mumbled prayer, and the rosary glided through her trembling fingers.

"Hey, you!" Turlupin cried in dismay. "I gave you an eight-sou piece, don't you see?"

The Trinitarian monk standing beside the church door gave a start and stared at Turlupin in surprise, but the old woman made no reply.

"She's not only blind but deaf to boot," Turlupin said angrily, and shrugged his shoulders. He deliberated for a while. Then, seeing that he could expect no intercession from the old woman, he decided to take his own just cause in hand.

Behind a column on the left-hand wall hung a picture representing the Adoration of the Lamb and the fulfilment of salvation. Apostles, popes, prophets and Old Testament patriarchs kneeled before a wellspring of living water while the Lamb's blood flowed into a golden chalice. The heavens had opened, and God the Father sat enthroned with the triple crown on his head and his hands raised in benediction. Mary, wearing a blue robe and bathed in sunlight, was seated on his right.

Turlupin went and stood in front of this picture, and his fervent prayer mingled with the words of the priest who was commending the dead man's soul to God's mercy.

"Don't listen to him," Turlupin entreated. "You mustn't believe all he told you about me. He's lying. I've always been a charitable sort, but that fellow's no beggar, he's a good-for-nothing, and his son squanders money on musicians and women. I gave the eight-sou piece to that old woman there. She deserves it – she's blind and deaf, as you can see."

But no sign of forgiveness emanated from the painted heaven.

God the Father continued to gaze down impassively at the apostles, the martyrs, the prophets, and Turlupin.

"God isn't listening," Turlupin whispered in dismay. "He believes that old peg-leg, not me."

In his heartfelt despair he remembered his vow and the candle under his arm. The candle – he simply had to placate God with the candle. He peered through the iron grille at the interior of the church, which was draped in black cloth and thronged with reverent worshippers. A thunderous *In resurrectionis gloria* was ascending to the domed roof. Many hundreds of candles – wax candles of red, yellow and blue – were burning on the high altar and in the aisles, and it was into that sea of radiance that his own poor flame must be plunged.

"There's nothing for it," he said miserably, "I shall have to have a Mass said for that worthless old man. God insists on it."

He turned to the Trinitarian monk standing beside the church door.

"Father," he said, "I've vowed to pay for a requiem Mass. Do you know the name of the old man they're burying in there?"

"Jean Gédéon, Duc de Lavan, of the house of La Tremouille," whispered the monk.

"Jean, Duc de . . . impossible!" cried Turlupin. "But I saw him begging on a bridge!"

"Jean Gédéon, Duc de Lavan, of the house of La Tremouille," the monk repeated, "Hereditary Governor of the Ile de France and Grand Master of the Horse to His Majesty, our most gracious lord and king."

"May he partake of Paradise," Turlupin muttered in dismay and bewilderment. Then, with hesitant tread, he stepped through the open ironwork door into the interior of the church, where the nobility of France had assembled.

[5]

SLOWLY, TURLUPIN TOOK stock of his surroundings. He saw the pomp and splendour of the court on all sides, heard the whisper of silk, the rustle of gold brocade and satin. Sashes, ribbons and silver lace abounded, as did necklaces of sparkling stones, hatbands, buckles and clasps. Swords clanked faintly on the church's flagstoned floor as the Lauds and Nocturns rang out from the choir. Exotic perfumes mingled with the scent of incense.

Turlupin perceived his mistake: no beggar's funeral could have occasioned all this pomp. Looking at the coffin on the catafalque, he saw that twelve candles of yellow wax were burning to right and left of it, saw the archbishop surrounded by his chaplains and altar boys. No, this was no modest Mass for a pauper. The doors from which steps led down into the crypt stood open, for the burial was to take place within the church itself, not in the graveyard. This convinced Turlupin that the dead man had truly been a duke, a peer of the realm, for he knew that burial within the church was a sacred prerogative of kings and popes, cardinals and members of the senior nobility.

The four noblemen chosen to carry the coffin down into the crypt stood there in solemn silence. Four pages dressed in black and violet held the corners of the pall, which was embroidered with silver thread. A manservant waited for the archbishop's signal to drape the coffin in an armorial coat, and behind him, bearing the late duke's spurs, plumed hat and sword, stood the steward of the house of Lavan.

"That monk in the vestibule was undoubtedly telling the truth," Turlupin said to himself, "so what am I doing here? Where in the world have they buried the beggar from the Pont- Rouge, and why was I directed here? Perhaps this isn't the Trinitarian church at all – there are so many churches, one can't be expected to remember them all. I know of another three in this quarter alone. There's St Polycarp's and the Ecce Homo, and the Carmelite church must also be somewhere in the neighbourhood – that monk outside looked like a Carmelite. Perhaps I'm in the Carmelite church. Of course! I'm in the Carmelite church – that explains everything."

He felt heartened and reassured by the thought that he was decently attired in his Sunday suit, like a man of good standing. He mustn't let anyone see his shoes, admittedly. They were patched, being his only pair.

When the choir had sung the *Magnificat* and the *Placebo*, he turned to an old gentleman standing beside him. "Sir," he said, "am I in the Trinitarian church or the church of the Carmelites?"

"In the Trinitarian church, sir, if it please you," replied the old man. "I, too, am here for the first time. I make confession at the church of the Discalced Friars and hear the Sunday sermon at Saint-Jacques de la Bougerie. Father Eustache preaches there."

"Remarkable," said Turlupin, who now knew where he was, and lapsed into silence.

"Truly remarkable," the old man went on. "The good Father is well over eighty years old. It's fifty-seven years since my own father first took me to Sunday service. The weather was snowy, and we drove there in a carriage upholstered with red velvet. It seems only yesterday. 'He's a great wag,' my father told me. 'He tells people what they have no wish to hear, but in the most agreeable way.' In those days Father Eustache still preached at the church of Saint-Blaise des Arcs."

The responsory came to an end. Quietly reciting the Paternoster, the archbishop approached the catafalque escorted on his right by two priests bearing the censer and aspersorium. The manservant holding the armorial coat suddenly bowed his head, and a stifled sob was heard.

The old gentleman beside Turlupin heaved a sigh. "Yes indeed," he said, "we've suffered a great loss. He meant everything to the king – he was our hope and protection. Now that he's no more, who will resist the onslaughts of Monsieur le Cardinal? I foresee evil days ahead, sir – evil days for us and for France in general."

The archbishop took the aspersorium from the priest and sprinkled the coffin, three times on the left side and three times on the right. Then he stationed himself in front of the crucifix and loudly intoned the *Ne nos inducas.*

As the throng of clerics and choristers withdrew to the south side of the altar, Turlupin caught sight of a lady in deepest mourning. She was standing behind the catafalque on the arm of a very young man, her veil half raised to reveal a proud, expressionless face that might have been carved in stone. She was leaning forward a little, and her eyes were staring at Turlupin with strange intensity. It was as if she could see him alone – him alone out of all the many hundreds of people that filled the church – and he trembled under her gaze.

"Sir!" he whispered to his neighbour. "Be good enough to tell me who she is, that lady beyond the coffin."

"What, sir, is it possible that you fail to recognize Madame de Lavan? That lady is the duchess, mourning the death of her husband – everyone knows her. And the youth at her side is the late duke's only son, the heir to his name."

"She sees that I don't belong here," Turlupin told himself in dismay. "My presence vexes her, and the look on her face bids me go. It's true, I suppose – I don't cut much of a figure among all these fine gentlemen – but is it my fault I was directed here? Very well, so be it, I'm going . . . "

And slowly, step by step, he proceeded to withdraw.

But he didn't get far. It was hard to thread his way through so many people. Those around him became restive and started whispering irately, so he decided to stay where he was.

"Go," he muttered, "why should I go? It's not my fault. I was wrongly informed, but now I'm here. Surely a church exists for the benefit of all?"

But the duchess's gaze continued to dwell on him. His uneasiness mounted. He turned his head and tried to avoid those eyes. Attentively, he studied the bronze relief over the entrance, the pilasters faced with lapis lazuli, the marble angels in the north aisle, the Coronation of the Virgin above the altar. The man in front of him sported puffed sleeves of yellow Chinese silk, and his neighbour on the left wore the blue sash of the Order of the Holy Ghost.

All this he saw, but he could simultaneously sense that the duchess's gaze still rested on him – that her eyes still held him in thrall. He shrugged. She ought to see how impossible it was for him to leave at present. Anyone would think it was easy! Damn it all, he couldn't simply soar into the air and vanish like the Holy Ghost!

All at once he felt something brush his neck and caught a momentary glimpse of a hand stealing over his shoulder. Turning, he found himself looking into the pallid face of a gaunt, elderly man, who promptly fell back a step. And then he noticed that his chain was gone – the chain he wore around his neck, the one with the medallion bearing his portrait and that of his employer.

Thief! The word flashed through his mind as he grabbed the wrist of the man he'd caught in the act. His captive's face wore a look of helpless consternation. He made no attempt to resist or escape; he simply raised his left hand in a pitiful gesture of entreaty.

At that moment Turlupin caught sight of the Duchesse de Lavan. She was still leaning forward and staring fixedly at him, but he thought he now detected a hint of suspense, of wild agitation, on her marble countenance. She gazed at the thief and at himself, never averting her eyes from what was in progress.

Under the impact of that gaze, Turlupin released the hand he was clutching. The man gave a deep sigh, then stepped to the left and instantly disappeared behind a column.

The four noblemen carried the coffin down the steps, followed by the congregation. As if awaking from a dream, Turlupin found himself alone in the spacious nave. And, while the strains of *In Paradisum* issued from the crypt, he strode, deep in thought, across the echoing flagstones and out into the open air.

[6]

STILL LOST IN thought, Turlupin made his way along the narrow, winding lanes that led from the Place de la Trinité to the banks of the Seine. He walked with bowed head, his shoulders brushing loose mortar from the walls as he went. He neither recognized those who passed him nor perceived that the rain was saturating his coat. He saw and noticed nothing. His innermost self resounded to the thunder of the organ and a solemn *Te Deum.*

His daydreams and vague suspicions had become reality: he had found his mother – she had seen and recognized him by the lock of white hair on his brow. Unable to call out or give him a sign, she had spoken with her eyes alone. Yes, now he understood the mute language of that gaze: "Is it you? Can it be? Are you really he? Where do you live and what name do you bear, my poor child?" Good mother! She had not been at liberty, with so many eyes upon her, to open her arms and obey the dictates of her heart. And so, not wishing to lose track of him again, she had sent her manservant to procure a portrait of her rediscovered son.

No, more than his portrait. Wasn't the same manservant following him at this very moment, charged with discovering where he lived and what he did? Turlupin had no need to turn his head; he knew that the man who had taken the medallion was following him, watching his every move – he could sense it and hear his footsteps.

Turlupin paused awhile. The significance of this moment was clear to him. His destiny must be determined before he reached home. It was still his to shape. He could master it – he could elect whether to go on leading his old, familiar life or venture forth upon a new and unfamiliar existence that seemed to him bright yet dark, alien yet predestined to be his from the hour of his birth onwards. And suddenly it occurred to him that his life hitherto had abounded in pleasant times, and that he had found happiness in the barbershop owned by the Widow Sabot, who loved him. And he could picture her sorrowful expression as he took leave of her. "Madame Sabot," he heard himself say, "rest assured that I shall never cease to think of you. My resolve to esteem you more highly than any other woman alive, not only now but in the future, is steadfast and unshakeable. Permit me to add, Madame . . ."

At that point his train of thought ended. He was overwhelmed with sadness and assailed by a sneaking desire that all might remain as it was, at least for a little while longer.

"He's dogging my footsteps," Turlupin muttered with a timid, sidelong glance, not daring to turn and look back. "Very well, he may be following me, but he hasn't caught me, not by a long chalk. In this neighbourhood, where I know every nook and cranny? Ridiculous!"

And with sudden decision he broke into a run, meaning to round the next corner, give his pursuer the slip, and evade the destiny which he had so often, so ardently invoked and craved, but which now confronted him with such imperious urgency.

But he didn't run far. A few steps, and he came to a halt.

It was as if two eyes were following him on his flight through the winding streets. He had a vision of a rigid, motionless, mournful face. The eyes had found him and were holding him fast under their reproachful gaze. "Would you flee from me, my son? Would you flee from me? Am I to lose you as soon as I have found you?"

Turlupin squared his shoulders, all hesitation gone. His mother was calling him. He must go to her, he must see her – it was the will of God, who had directed him to the Trinitarian church so that the preordained course of destiny might be fulfilled in him.

But yesterday's happiness crept up on him once more, beguiling him. His mind's eye conjured up the image of little Nicole, of whom he was so fond. Every evening, when work was over for the day, she would bring him his measure of wine from the Taverne des Apôtres. He saw her scampering across the twilit street with her dress hitched up and two copper sous in her hand, saw Jamine the cat scamper after her, saw Madame Sabot rinsing the dishes in warm water while singing a song from her grandmother's girlhood:

When in Le Havre I used to dwell,
my sweetheart taught me how to dance.
He kissed my lips at every step,
and Cupid smiled on our romance.

Turlupin sighed. His eyes grew moist, and a feeling of infinite regret stole over him. But all at once, as he stood there wavering and wrestling with his emotions, the vision of little Nicole vanished, to be replaced by that of the Duc de Lavan's coffin on its black catafalque. The dim figures of priests and altar boys moved round it like shadows, the silver crucifix glittered on the candlelit altar. In a flash, Turlupin knew that the illustrious duke had been his father. Father . . . The meaning of the word struck home for the very first time in his life. He was suddenly appalled to think that he had attended his father's funeral like an unconcerned, indifferent stranger. Only now did the mournful solemnity of that occasion dawn on him. He pictured the four noblemen as they swayed along before him with the duke's coffin on their shoulders, flanked by four pages clad in black and violet. He himself occupied that place in the cortège to which his rank entitled him: he, the heir to the name, grief-stricken but with head erect, was walking behind the banner and standard of the house of La Tremouille, while a full-throated *In resurrectionis gloria* soared heavenwards on every side.

Little Nicole, who had been keeping watch for Turlupin outside the door of the barbershop, caught sight of him coming down the Rue des Apôtres. He was walking with measured tread behind an imaginary coffin, one hand resting on the pommel of an invisible sword.

"There you are at last, Monsieur Turlupin!" she cried. "Look sharp, run, they're waiting for you!"

And, at the sound of her familiar voice, the first-born son of the Duc de Lavan transformed himself into Turlupin the wig-maker, who ran, with the utmost alacrity, to rejoin his razors, pomade pots and curling tongs.

[7]

HE DUCKED TO avoid hitting his nose on the wooden head that hung above the barbershop door, exposed to the wind and rain, to signify that second-hand wigs, too, were purchased and made-over on the premises, Turlupin having learned how to fashion one new wig out of two old ones.

"Your humble servant, Monsieur Turlupin!" called Monsieur Pigeot, the dyer, whose workshop was next door. "You know how to while away the time, eh? You go for a stroll, greet your friends, prattle and gossip – yes, and what about my wig, eh?"

Monsieur Pigeot was perched on the big copper drum used for drying hair. His sturdy legs were too short to reach the floor, and he had covered his bald pate with the Widow Sabot's floorcloth. This, coupled with his indigo-stained hands and his choice of seat, lent him the curiously exotic appearance of one who had just arrived in Paris from the Barbary Coast.

The barbershop was crowded. Monsieur Froisset, a parliamentarian's clerk, was pacing up and down with an irritable, morose expression. Monsieur Gaspard, the clothier's assistant from the Rue de Froment, sat quietly musing in a corner with Jamine the cat stretched out at his feet, the red blotches on his gaunt cheeks just visible in the fading light of the bleak autumn day. The landlord of the Taverne des Apôtres was seated astride the bench near the stove with his left leg knee-deep in a bucket of warm sand, the physician having prescribed a dry bath for his gouty foot. To pass the time, he had challenged the vicar of St Polycarp's to Toccadilla, a board-and-dice game.

Madame Sabot was at the plaiting board, braiding chestnut hair into thin strands. Looking over her shoulder at the movements of her nimble fingers was Monsieur Le Gouche, an impoverished Picard nobleman who had taken refuge from his creditors in a garret in the house next door. At home he had neither candlelight nor a warm stove; here in the Widow Sabot's barbershop he could enjoy both.

"There it is," Turlupin told Monsieur Pigeot, pointing to a straw-coloured peruke hanging on the wall. "I've already finished the upper part, the big curls, side curls and hairline. All that's left to do is the cow-lick – oh yes, and the smaller curls too."

"There's horsehair in it," said Monsieur Pigeot, peering closely at the wig.

The Widow Sabot's hands came to a momentary stop. "Sir," she protested, "don't even mention horsehair, the very word saddens me. We never use horsehair – it's dull and brittle."

"Come, now," exclaimed Monsieur Le Gouche. "If you think all horsehair is brittle, fair lady, you're much mistaken. I think I can claim to know a thing or two about horses. You should have seen my carriage horses, a pair of dapple-greys with manes as soft as goat hair."

"Goat hair is no use either," the widow told him. "Only human hair will do for wigs. The best comes from Normandy – that's because the women there wear bonnets all the time. The less hair is exposed to fresh air, the easier it is to curl."

"Four and three make seven," said the landlord of the Taverne des Apôtres. "Reverend Father, kindly leave your mouse where it is, I have another throw to come."

The dyer, who had meantime clapped the wig on his head, emitted a bellow of complaint.

"It doesn't fit! One puff of wind will send it flying! I'll be the laughingstock of the entire neighbourhood."

"Upon my soul, he's right," Monsieur Le Gouche chimed in.

"It'll stay put, sir, it'll stay put," Turlupin exclaimed in alarm. "I measured you from temple to temple and crown to neck. Bear in mind, sir, that a wig takes time to accommodate itself to the head. What's more, it isn't finished yet."

"Damnation!" cried the taverner. "My back aches from sitting so long. I haven't slept, either. I paid a call on a young woman last night. Her husband returned unexpectedly, so I had to retire to the attic. I spent the night between two bundles of thatch, with only a cat for company."

"You're overfond of women," said the widow. "It's bad for your gout."

The taverner's face contorted itself into a grimace of pain and self-satisfaction.

"I have a host of troubles to contend with by day," he said, "not to mention the pain in my leg. I want some pleasure *some* time."

"Your remarks are depraved in the extreme," the vicar rebuked him. "You'd do better to attend to the game. You ought to be ashamed of yourself."

Turlupin had finally succeeded in placating Monsieur Pigeot. Much relieved, he turned to Monsieur Gaspard.

"At your service, sir. I await your orders."

Monsieur Gaspard rose. Startled out of its slumbers, the cat made for the taverner, but the taverner disliked cats. Remembering his companion of the previous night, he raised his sound leg and prepared to give it a kick.

The cat ran off, the taverner continued to bemoan his lot.

"Jesus, my leg! Ten thousand devils have set about this leg of mine – it's unendurable. For four days now I've attended church each morning and entreated God for some fine, dry weather, because the pain is worse than ever in all this wet, but what's the use of praying? It rains every day."

"My son," the vicar said mildly, "if God were to grant all our requests, France would be in a sorry state."

"I have an ointment for you, sir," Turlupin was heard to say. "It renders the skin smooth and supple, and it costs but three blancs."

The taverner and the vicar were now engrossed in their game. Monsieur Froisset continued to pace the room with a grim and malevolent expression. The nobleman from Picardy ran his hand lightly over the widow's plump, rosy arm.

"Madame," he said, "today I was invited to dine with an old friend of mine, Monsieur de Chavigny. He's a great scholar, and devotes himself exclusively to the study of natural phenomena. He also keeps an excellent table. There was, among other things, a *ragoût chasseur*. Are you familiar with that dish?"

"*Ragoût chasseur*!" the widow cried ecstatically, revelling in memories. "For that one needs a piece of veal, a thin slice of ham, and a partridge's wing. Then an egg for the gravy, butter for braising the sliced meat, some onions, vinegar, mustard, and a little Burgundy wine."

"Not onions, Madame," Monsieur Le Gouche protested.

"Yes indeed, onions too. Half an ounce – a quarter, perhaps. Little more than a pinch."

"There!" cried the taverner. "I've broken through your line – I'm advancing."

"Ham! Veal! Partridges' wings!" the parliamentarian's clerk exclaimed bitterly. "Oh yes, the gentry know how to live. They loll around in their mansions, feasting, while the likes of us . . . "He broke off. "Shall I tell you what I was served for breakfast today? A slice of bread and treacle!"

"Treacle is sovereign for purifying the blood," said the widow.

"What nonsense!" cried the taverner. "It's as good as proved that eating treacle gives you tapeworms in the guts."

"Ah," said Monsieur Le Gouche, "I suppose that you, Monsieur Froisset, would like to breakfast every day on milk soup and biscuits followed by a piece of game pie, well truffled and not too small."

"Folk are quite unaware how choice and precious a gift of God bread is," the vicar remarked. "It's cheap and they eat it every day – that's why they don't appreciate its worth as they should. There are no farmers at home in the village where I was born, only woodcutters. They see no bread from one year's end to the next; they live on burdock and sow-thistle roots, likewise on swedes, which they consume raw, yet they remain hale and hearty enough to tote their loads down the mountainside for five hours at a time, nor do they retire to the almshouse at Jean de Maurienne till they're eighty years old."

"Do you really believe," Monsieur Gaspard's horrified voice broke in abruptly, " – do you really believe, Reverend Father, that God has destined those men to live like beasts of burden and die in a poorhouse? What a state of affairs, by heaven! All men come into the world with an equal right to happiness, don't you understand that?"

The vicar of St Polycarp's did not reply, for the game was now claiming his full attention, but Monsieur Gaspard's words had aroused the displeasure of the Picard nobleman.

"Bravo, sir," he cried, "you parrot your lesson excellently. One hears it on every street corner these days. It's the precept of that wily old philosopher whom one often sees depicted at the feet of St Michael – you know who I mean. No, sir, in France good order prevails in all things, and I wish for none better. There have been rich and poor, hungry and replete, in every age."

"What you call good order," Monsieur Gaspard said meditatively, as Turlupin shaved his chin, "I call the brutal tyranny of the stronger. For whom was it created, this good order of yours? I'll tell you: For the twelve hundred highwaymen who, with the king's consent, have shared out everything among themselves, posts and offices, happiness and prosperity."

"Bend your head back, Monsieur Gaspard," murmured Turlupin.

"Have a care, sir!" Monsieur Le Gouche said in meaningful tones. "I've no wish to hear such talk, upon my honour as a nobleman. People have been transported for less to Florida or Guadeloupe, and that's a voyage that doesn't agree with everyone."

As if his thoughts had strayed to the far-off islands of the West, Monsieur Gaspard stared pensively at the barbershop's smoke-stained ceiling.

"Let them send me to Guadeloupe," he said. "What would it matter? *Coelum, non animum, mutant qui trans mare currunt.* Even under a foreign sky, I should remain the man I am."

"As you will," said Monsieur Le Gouche. "I know no Latin, but mark this, sir: a man can also be whipped and flogged for such talk."

In token that he considered the conversation at an end, he turned to the Widow Sabot. "You, Madame," he said, indicating her bosom, "possess a barricade I would gladly storm, were my sword not rusty and I myself not getting on in years."

"You're too kind, sir," said the widow, without looking up from her work.

Just then the door burst open and little Nicole appeared on the threshold accompanied by a giant of a man in the costume of a Seine bargee. She was holding him by the hem of his coat and doing her best to drag him into the room.

"Come in, Monsieur," she cried eagerly in her piping voice. "Why hesitate? Your every wish will be attended to here. No one knows his trade better than Monsieur Turlupin."

The man looked down at Nicole's diminutive figure, seemingly unable to get his bearings. Then he doffed his cap to the taverner, whom he for some reason assumed to be the owner of the establishment.

"The two of us," he said, "that's to say, my comrade and I, were standing outside, waiting for Monsieur de Saint-Chéron, for we're bidden to conduct him to his friends, who are awaiting him he knows where. He cannot be allowed to go unescorted, you understand – not after what happened last Friday. Then this little girl appeared."

He stooped and, with the greatest care, detached Nicole's fingers from his coat-tail.

"You say you're waiting for Monsieur de Saint-Chéron?" exclaimed Monsieur Le Gouche. "Is that the man whose orders are being passed from street to street? Where is he? Where can I find him, and what's all this talk about St Martin's Day? Everyone speaks of it. I'd give a great deal to set eyes on this Monsieur de Saint-Chéron."

The Seine bargeman stared at him in bewilderment. He seemed to deliberate, his lips moving silently. Then, all at once, he let out a bellow of laughter.

"You wish to see Monsieur de Saint-Chéron? You jest! Listen to this, Jacob! Hey, Jacob, come in! There's someone here wishes to see Monsieur de Saint-Chéron. That's really droll!"

"Silence, you numskull!" said a voice from the street. "Come out, you blabbermouth! All you can do is open and shut that trap of yours."

A bearded face appeared behind the bargee, and a huge rudder-stock came into view. The object of the newcomer's reprimand stood there for a moment with his mouth open, thoroughly perplexed. Then he came to a decision: he turned about and marched off into the darkness without another word.

"Strange fellows, those," said Monsieur Le Gouche. "They've been a common sight in the streets for quite a while now. They're agitated for some reason. Better they should remain aboard their vegetable boats – they're as clumsy as turtles when they're not afloat on the Seine."

Monsieur Gaspard rose, and, while Turlupin was smoothing his coat down, deposited two sous on Madame Sabot's counter. Then, with a bow to all present, he left the barbershop as silently and discreetly as ever.

The taverner limped to the door in his wake, leaning on the arm of his friend the vicar. This was the moment for which Turlupin had been waiting. The matter he wished to discuss with Monsieur Froisset was not for everyone's ears.

[8]

TURLUPIN WENT UP to the parliamentarian's clerk and bowed with the greatest respect.

"If you please, sir," he said, "I'm entirely at your service."

With a martyred air, Monsieur Froisset seated himself on one of the chairs and acquainted Turlupin with his wishes.

"But be quick," he commanded, "it's devilish uncomfortable, sitting here. Trim it ear-length on the right and shoulder-length on the left."

Turlupin reached for the scissors and the broad comb.

"With a cut of that sort," he said, "you shouldn't wear your old rabbitskin cap. What suits that cut is a broad-brimmed hat with a long feather in it."

Monsieur Froisset took great offence at this advice. He was determined to go on wearing his old cap until his employer, the parliamentarian, presented him with another.

"All right, all right," he muttered irritably. "Haven't you anything else of interest to tell me?"

"Upon my soul, I do indeed," Turlupin whispered eagerly, "but it's a great secret. You'll never believe it, Monsieur Froisset. Listen to this: a noblewoman – perhaps you can guess who I mean – "

"Louder!" said Monsieur Froisset. "I didn't catch a word."

"Very well, I'll begin again," Monsieur Le Gouche called from the other end of the room. "I was just telling Madame Sabot that, in the last year of the late king's reign, my tenants used to sell a sucking pig for seventeen sous. Today, a boiling fowl costs precisely the same sum. That's all I said."

"In short, a duchess," Turlupin pursued in an undertone. "Her marriage produced a son whose existence she conceals from the world at large."

"What's that to me?" said Monsieur Froisset.

"But it's remarkable, no?"

"There's nothing remarkable about it," declared the parliamentarian's clerk. "Such cases are not unknown. There was a time when it was dangerous for many a great lord to possess a male heir. I myself once knew a Huguenot nobleman who – "

"But this son," Turlupin broke in, "is aware of his origins and determined to claim his due."

"Ah, that's another matter," said Monsieur Froisset, swiftly calculating how much he and his employer could make out of such a suit. "That's an extremely complicated case – one that falls within the competence of Parliament. If Parliament were to recognize him . . . "

Turlupin stood there scissors in hand, smiling happily with his eyes shut. His imagination had conjured up a parchment adorned with a red wax seal suspended from a ribbon of green silk.

"It isn't easy, of course," the clerk went on. "Any suit presented to Parliament must be supported by evidence. Whatever submission the petitioner may make, the immediate and universal response is: 'Your evidence, sir, submit your evidence.'"

"And what must he do to obtain his due?"

"The first step is to procure an extract from the baptismal register," Monsieur Froisset explained. "That costs money. Next, two advocates, one of the Robe and one of the Sword. Them he can also acquire for money. Finally, there are the compurgators and witnesses."

"Witnesses?" Turlupin said in a strangled voice. "Where would he find witnesses in such a case?"

"He'll find witnesses enough if he has money," the clerk replied. "That's quite simple."

Turlupin completed his work in a mood of deep depression. Money? He had none. He debated what he could quickly convert into money. His Sunday suit was worth twelve livres. The little silver crucifix was another possibility. There were also the feather bed and the tapestry in the bedroom upstairs, the one depicting Queen Judith, but both those articles, the feather bed and the tapestry, belonged to Madame Sabot, not to him.

"Money?" Turlupin said quietly and apprehensively. "He has none."

The clerk waxed indignant. "No money? Why didn't you say so at once? If he has no money, his suit is as good as lost."

Turlupin laid aside the scissors and comb.

"He's a poor man," he said forlornly. "Where would he find the money?"

"That's his affair, not mine," retorted the clerk. "Five thousand livres, that's the very minimum."

"And I thought a lock of white hair would be sufficient," Turlupin muttered despondently.

Monsieur Froisset rose and retrieved his cap, but he didn't go; he stood there, thinking hard. Suddenly he put his arm round Turlupin's shoulder and drew him into a corner.

"You should write and tell her that you know everything," he said in a low, confidential tone.

"Write? To whom should I write?" Turlupin demanded.

"Being privy to her secret, you could put it to good use."

Turlupin's incomprehension persisted, so the clerk made his meaning plainer.

"She should pay for our silence, that's all."

"Monsieur Froisset!" hissed Turlupin, turning pale with horror at this scheme. "You're a miserable wretch. Not another word – I'll hear no more of it!"

The parliamentarian's clerk made one more attempt to gain Turlupin's support for his idea by appealing to common sense. "I don't understand you," he said."Why not improve your lot? Why should you give a fig for that miserly, scrawny, overdressed old bitch?"

"Who?" cried Turlupin.

"The duchess, of course."

"By God," Turlupin bellowed, "this is too much!"

He drew himself up. As if in a dream, he saw again his mother's regal, awe-inspiring figure, the grief-transfigured countenance, the eyes that had sought him out. This man had insulted her. Sensing that the noble spirit of his ancestors had awakened within him, he knew how he must comport himself.

"Sir," he told the parliamentarian's clerk in an icy voice, "I infer but one thing from all you have said, namely, that you desire to see me sword in hand."

"Did you hear what's afoot, Madame?" cried Monsieur Le Gouche. "A duel by torchlight! A duel between a clerk and a barber – capital! This promises to be amusing."

"Jesus, Monsieur Turlupin!" shrieked the widow, and Monsieur Froisset spoke at almost the same moment. "To see you with a sword in your hand, you buffoon," he declared, "would be a paltry pleasure."

"I demand satisfaction," Turlupin told him doggedly.

"You demand satisfaction?" sneered the clerk. "You shall have it. You cut my hair, you dolt. Here are two sous. That's the only satisfaction I owe you. If I think fit, you knucklehead, I shall write to her myself."

"Ah!" yelled Turlupin. "That's enough!"

He hurled himself at Monsieur Froisset, but the clerk eluded him, vaulted over the table, and blew out both candles in a trice.

The ensuing darkness was rent by the sound of overturned chairs and a shattered washbowl, by the widow's cries for help and Turlupin's triumphant voice.

"Got you at last, you fool! Just wait, you won't escape me again!"

"Ouch!" cried Monsieur le Gouche. "You're very strong, my lad, but release my arm or I'll be obliged to box your ears."

At the same instant, the clerk's voice came from the other side of the room.

"Show yourself, you wet sponge! Come here, you lily-livered lout! I'll teach you to pick a quarrel with me! I'll slit you up the middle with a fishbone!"

"I'll throttle you!" growled Turlupin, laying about him in the gloom with the sand bucket, the vice, the ash can, the broom, and the hair drum. "I'll break every bone in your body!"

"He'll throttle him, do you hear, Monsieur Le Gouche?" wailed the widow. "He'll break every bone in his body. Separate them, for God's sake!"

All at once, a glimmer of light illuminated the hurly-burly. Little Nicole, swathed in a sheet and carrying a stump of candle, emerged from the inner chamber that served the widow as store-room, bedroom and kitchen.

"What happened, Monsieur Turlupin?" she asked plaintively. "What have you done with my cat? Jamine, my poor little Jamine, I can't see you. Where are you?"

Turlupin stood panting amid the havoc he had wrought. He peered about him for his adversary, but the clerk had seized his chance as soon as the light appeared and was already outside in the street. Knowing himself to be safe, he pointed a scornful yet pitying finger at the grazed, dishevelled, breathless figure of Turlupin, who was standing in the candelight with a bruise on his forehead and ash all over his face.

"Just look at him, Madame," said Monsieur Froisset. "Isn't it sad to think that Christ died for that imbecile, too?"

A wooden wig-stand sailed across the barbershop but missed its mark, for Monsieur Froisset had already made off. Turlupin, who raced to the door with the curling tongs in his hand, ready to commit murder, got there just in time to see him disappear round the next corner.

Madame Sabot tearfully gathered up the fragments of her washbowl. Little Nicole, shivering with cold in her sheet, sat down on the bench by the stove and hugged her cat, which had reappeared. Monsieur Le Gouche was rubbing his arm.

"If he dares to write to her," muttered Turlupin, feeling utterly wretched, "I'll split his skull for him. He doesn't know her name, that's the lucky part. He'd better not show his face here again, or I'll . . . "

He broke off and stood there like a graven image. The curling tongs slipped through his fingers and fell to the floor. A gust of wind wafted across the room, tousled Monsieur Pigeot's wig, and plucked at the sheet covering the weary little girl, who had already fallen asleep on the bench.

Turlupin swung round abruptly. He reached Madame Sabot in a single stride and drew her to the door.

"Look there!" he said, beside himself with excitement. "She came in person – she was here. The clerk was lying. It isn't true, what he said about money and witnesses and evidence. She came in person, so she now knows where to find me. Ah, Madame, things are taking their course. I need no money or witnesses. I'm very happy, Madame, very happy indeed."

And, holding the widow's hand in a vicelike grip, he pointed to a carriage that was slowly and laboriously rumbling along the Rue des Douze Apôtres.

[9]

TURLUPIN SET TO work early next morning as if nothing had happened. On entering the barbershop with his breakfast of bread and milk, the widow found him already seated at the vice. He had arranged the locks of hair for Monsieur Pigeot's wig in order of length and was anointing them with a little olive oil to render them smooth and supple. The work appeared to be claiming all his attention. He didn't look up and said he didn't mind if the milk went cold; he had no time to spare. He was afraid the widow would ply him with questions and reproaches, nor could he forgive her the fact that, in last night's extremity of joy and happiness, he had almost betrayed his secret to her. As long as he could feel her troubled, anxious gaze upon him, Monsieur Pigeot's yellow wig remained the most important thing in the world. Once she had left the room, however, he laid aside the curling tongs and surrendered himself to his thoughts. And, while he was staring into space like a sleepwalker, the everyday things around him vanished – table, bench, stove, iron fire-dogs, barber's implements – and his mind's eye envisioned the ponderous, majestic carriage of the house of La Tremouille rumbling through the tortuous streets to transport him from the bleak confines of his present life to the great and splendid destiny that lay in store for him.

But the day wore on, and no word came from the Duchesse de Lavan. Late that night, when the barbershop had been vacated by its last customer, an indigent weaver whom the widow permitted to have his beard trimmed gratis once a month for the love of God and the forgiveness of her sins, Turlupin took his Sunday suit from the chest and bade Madame Sabot farewell.

"I must go," he said, looking down at the floor. "I'm only waiting for the rain to ease a little."

"You're going out?" the widow exclaimed in dismay, filled with dark forebodings. Turlupin had never before left the house so late. He would sit on the bench beside the stove, night after night, sipping his measure of wine and reading *The Seal of Wisdom*. "You're going out? At this hour and in this weather?"

Turlupin cast an uneasy glance at his new suit. "It's true, the rain won't stop before daybreak. I don't want to go, but what's the use? I've received my orders and I must obey."

"I really don't know why you should set such store by Monsieur Vauquelin's orders," the widow said heatedly. "Let him attend to the selling of his apple wine himself. Or is it his daughter that gives you orders? If so, of course, I fully understand your eagerness."

"Madame," Turlupin assured her, "Monsieur Vauquelin is quite as unknown to me as his daughter or his apple wine. My orders are of a different nature. I've been summoned by God Himself."

"You don't know Monsieur Vauquelin?" snapped the widow. "You expect me to believe that? Why, yesterday evening, when he passed by . . . "

She broke off. Her face conveyed hurt surprise, her eyes brimmed with tears.

"The medallion, Monsieur Turlupin – where's the medallion? Didn't you promise me to treasure it? Has God, whose name you've just employed to cloak your evil designs – has He also forbidden you to wear the medallion that bore my likeness and yours?"

Turlupin put a hand to his chest.

"The medallion?" he muttered in consternation. "You're right, I don't have it."

His face suddenly cleared.

"The medallion?" he repeated. "Ah yes, Madame, the chain snapped last night, while I was tussling in the dark with that swine of a clerk. I took it to the silversmith first thing this morning. He asked three sous."

Turlupin fell silent, realizing that he had fled from one predicament into another of even greater magnitude. If the widow took it into her head to inquire the silversmith's name, he would be in a dire dilemma. He let his hand fall and gazed into her face with fearful expectancy.

But, just at that moment, Monsieur Coquereau the grocer appeared in the doorway. He was soaked to the skin and out of breath, having run to the barbershop in his dripping shoes. Madame Sabot, who found this interruption most unwelcome, greeted him with only passing courtesy.

"There you are, Monsieur Coquereau," she said. "So the rain hasn't kept you away. How nice." Then, unable to suppress her annoyance altogether, she added, "You offer me tokens of your friendship almost daily, it seems."

"Madame," Monsieur Coquereau said with dignity, "I have the honour to pay you my respects."

He draped his coat over the back of a chair and drew it up to the fire. Meantime, Turlupin stole out of the door. He knew in that instant that he would never return to the Widow Sabot's barbershop. While slowly closing the door behind him, he took a long, last, farewell look at those features of his life which had hitherto been most precious to him: the book entitled *The Seal of Wisdom* and the sleeping form of little Nicole.

"He has really gone," the widow said sadly. "He wouldn't listen to me."

"A somewhat uncouth suitor," observed Monsieur Coquereau, who was drying his legs at the stove.

"Ah, Monsieur Coquereau, how sorely you misjudge him!" cried the widow. "You don't know him, believe me. He possesses a noble, generous nature and the finest manners in the world."

"Except, I regret to say, that he's off his head," said Monsieur Coquereau. "He's also the biggest fool in Christendom. Believe it or not, he came to my shop last week for no reason other than to tell me that he now knew there were twenty-four Princes of Hell, and that he was acquainted with the name of each."

"He read that in his book – a Carmelite priest left it behind, together with a poem in praise of St Louis. It's true, though, Monsieur Turlupin can be very odd at times. Last night he gaped at Monsieur Vauquelin's old carriage as if it held some miraculous significance for him, the Lord alone knows what. Monsieur Vauquelin leaves his village for the city twice a year to find a buyer for his apple wine and visit his daughter, who's married to Monsieur Lescalopier."

"I know Madame Lescalopier," Monsieur Coquereau chimed in. "She's from the country, and rumour has it that she cried out with feigned reluctance on her wedding night."

"Nowadays she deceives her husband," the widow went on, "which is only as much as he deserves. He's a vain, stupid nincompoop – not that her wits are any sharper than his."

Her thoughts returned to Turlupin. She was now more than ever convinced that he had become ensnared by Madame Lescalopier. Monsieur Coquereau likewise considered this a certainty.

"I, too," he said, "have suffered base ingratitude at the hands of a person dear to me. Yes, Madame, I loved her, and I should be most unworthy of the honour of your friendship were I to conceal it from you. Yes, she failed to appreciate the merits of a sensible, respectable husband endowed with a secure livelihood."

For a while neither spoke. Then Monsieur Coquereau proceeded to ply the widow with confidential information about his circumstances, his person, and his predilections.

"A secure livelihood I do have, thanks be to God. It's not so easy to keep a grocer's shop, Madame Sabot, but, say what you will, it provides a living. Everyone has need of pepper and saffron, oil and vinegar. Not to be cheated when buying merchandise, that's what counts. Selling it is a matter of course."

He put his arm round the widow's waist and drew her close.

"It's hard to find a wife who's pretty and goodnatured and not too old, as well as being adept at business. Not every woman possesses all those qualities combined. She would also have to amuse me, because I incline, as you know, to melancholy."

[10]

Meanwhile, out in the pouring rain, Turlupin was negotiating the sandy hillocks and stretches of grass that ran between the ramparts and the river. The night was dark, but he knew the way. He had discovered from the servant of a notary resident in the district that the Duc de Lavan's mansion was situated in the suburb of Suresnes, beyond the two flour mills and not far from the timber bridge that led to the Île de St Vincent.

A dank wind smote him in the face, but he held his coat together with both hands and pressed on, dominated by a single thought: he must see his mother before the night was out. Loath to wait any longer, he kept repeating, over and over again, "She has my picture, so I want hers." Those words steeled his resolve. They made him strong and gave him the courage his venture demanded.

The moon, briefly emerging from behind the clouds, revealed the flour mills, which seemed to Turlupin to rise directly from the swirling waters of the Seine. Then the path veered inland, and he glimpsed, scattered across the plain, the dark shapes of the houses of Suresnes, and, overtopping them all in their midst, the ducal mansion of the Lavans.

The massive building, flanked by two projecting corner turrets, loomed up beyond a broad expanse of grass with a well at its centre. Turlupin made out a flight of stone steps, a long row of brightly lit windows, and, above the portal, the arms of the house of

La Tremouille: a mailed fist surmounted by a fess and two thistles.

For a while he stood leaning against the parapet of the well. He saluted the coat of arms carved above the gate, convinced that he was not seeing it for the first time. The longer he stood there, the more certain he became that he had never forgotten this house – that he had preserved a vague, shadowy recollection of its appearance down the years. A momentary image from the furthermost recesses of his childhood flitted through his head: a wintry, snow-covered square, a carriage upholstered in red velvet, and himself being driven to Mass beside the majestic, stern-faced man who was his father.

A church clock struck eleven. Turlupin had the illusory sense that one of the illuminated windows was about to open, and that a slender white hand would beckon him inside. He straightened up: the time had come. With measured tread he crossed the open ground, and with measured tread he climbed the steps to the door. Then he rapped on it twice, demanding admittance to his ancestral home.

Voices approached, keys rattled, and the door creaked open. Someone shone a lantern on Turlupin's face. Two footmen were barring his path.

"Your name, sir?"

"I shall tell it to Madame la Duchesse," Turlupin replied.

The light travelled downwards from his lock of white hair to his patched shoes.

"What's your business with Madame?" asked the man with the lantern.

"Madame la Duchesse will learn that from my own lips," Turlupin said haughtily, confident that his words would have the desired effect.

"What impudence!" called a clear, youthful voice from inside the house. "That's not one of the guests we're expecting. It must be one of *his* minions! Give the fellow a sound thrashing and tell him to tell his master – "

A cudgel struck Turlupin's shoulder, then his arm, and a blow in the chest sent him reeling backwards. The door swung to with a crash. Turlupin stood there in the darkness, beside himself with rage, humiliation, and despair.

"They wouldn't let me see her!" he hissed in a choking whisper. "Those scoundrelly servants thrashed me. Where's my coat? Damn those accursed lackeys! Thrash me, would they? I won't forget that!"

Tears sprang to his eyes. He laughed loudly, harshly, at the absurdity of fate. To think that some festivity was in progress up there while he, the true Duc de Lavan, was standing outside in the rain, looking up at the lighted windows.

"She refuses to admit me to her presence," he whispered bitterly. "She's afraid to see me again. I'm to keep the secret to myself – I'm to remain Turlupin. Very well, but she has my picture and I want hers. I demand my due, nothing more."

He reviewed the situation. It wouldn't be hard to gain admittance to the house by day, when a horde of servants would surely be coming and going all the while. Tomorrow, then. Till then he must wait, but where? It was very cold. He had no wish to return to the barbershop, so where? Back to the river and beneath the wooden bridge? There were bound to be rats there, and he could see no sign of a stable or barn close at hand.

And then, barely twenty paces to his right, he caught sight of some steps leading up to a sacred image in a niche in the garden wall, and above this was a little roof. The wooden canopy would shelter him from the rain, and he might even be able to lie at full length.

But half-way there he came to an abrupt halt, seized with rage and resentment. He now knew the cause of his misfortune: seated on the steps, huddled up in his coat, was a beggar.

[11]

A BEGGAR – ONE of the base brotherhood of divine spies, one of those insatiable creatures that batten on respectable folk – had sat waiting on the steps for alms, even at night, and Turlupin had failed to see him. He had walked straight past without giving him a sou, and the wretch had cursed Turlupin in his mindless greed and malevolence; he had complained to God, and God had believed his calumnies and permitted those footmen to drive him, Turlupin, from the threshold of his own home.

Turlupin cast a sorrowful glance at the dark rain clouds scudding across the sky. Then he felt in his pocket for a coin, but all he found were some onions and a hunk of bread. He tossed the bread to the beggar.

"There," he said, "take it and leave me in peace."

The beggar did not stir. The bread, which had landed on the bottom step, continued to lie there untouched.

"No trickery, damn you!" Turlupin growled in dismay. "Take that bread and put it in your pouch, do you hear? You cannot say now that I showed you no compassion. Bread is as good a gift as money." The beggar still did not move. "Oh, so you don't want it?"

Stung by such sinful arrogance, Turlupin raised his eyes to heaven and, in his turn, complained of the beggar to God.

"You saw? He doesn't want bread, he's after money. Bread isn't good enough for this reprobate, yet you bent an ear to him – you let them beat me for his sake! I have no money – not a single sou, believe me, only this bread and three little onions, and earlier tonight, in the darkness, I failed to see him. I've been unjustly treated, do you hear? It's me, it's Turlupin who's addressing you."

The wind sent raindrops swirling into Turlupin's face. Just as he was vainly striving to shield himself with the hem of his coat, the beggar stood up.

"Sir," the man called, shouting to make himself heard above the whistle of the wind, "I saw everything. They drove you away in the most unseemly manner. From that I infer you to be an honest, trustworthy person."

Frozen with astonishment, Turlupin let go of his coat and peered into the darkness. This was no beggar's mode of speech. The man spoke like one accustomed to giving orders. Why, if he wasn't a beggar, had he been sitting on the rainswept steps beneath the figure of a saint?

"Who are you, sir?" Turlupin demanded. "Have you no home, that you sit here in the wind and the rain?"

The unknown man drew Turlupin beneath the wooden canopy.

"I am employed by a great lord whose name I am not at liberty to disclose," he said. "It was on his behalf that I was sitting here on watch. What of you, sir? You were disgracefully treated. Whom in the house of Lavan did you wish to see?"

"I had business with Madame la Duchesse," Turlupin replied, "but they wouldn't let me in."

"Madame la Duchesse, eh? What if it were possible for me to get you into the house?"

"They would give me another drubbing," Turlupin said glumly.

"Leave it to me," said the unknown man. "They won't beat you again – indeed, they'll receive you with the utmost courtesy."

Turlupin cast a worried glance at the front door. He thought awhile.

"If I can be assured of a better reception than I got the first time," he said at length, "and if you were really generous enough to do me such a favour, without even knowing me – "

"I'm most anxious to satisfy your requirements," said the stranger. "There's a condition attached, true, but I've no doubt you'll be willing to meet it. Nothing could be easier from your point of view. Come with me, sir, and all will be well."

"I'm coming," said Turlupin. While the stranger was going on ahead, he surreptitiously stooped to retrieve and pocket the piece of bread.

They made for the river and proceeded a fair way along the bank, which was thickly overgrown. Then their route led down to the water. The wind was moaning in the reeds, and its monotonous song combined with the gurgle of the sluggishly flowing river to produce a single, doleful melody.

A ferryman's hut took shape in the gloom. Turlupin's guide came to a halt and rapped on the wooden shutters.

"Open up, Pox-face!" he called. "It's me."

The door was opened by a tall, bearded man with pockmarked cheeks, and they entered a room of which only part was illumined by the reddish glow of a sullen fire. Fishing nets, large and small, hung from the low ceiling and cast weird, flickering shadows on the walls. Turlupin stole a glance at his companion. The man he had mistaken in the darkness for a beggar was attired like a scrivener: black gown, white ruff, ink bottle and quills at his belt. As fleshless as a stick of firewood, he had a misshapen body and an ochre face imprinted with a multitude of little wrinkles.

He had gone over to the fire and was warming his hands at it. A pig emerged from the shadows and rubbed its snout against Turlupin's patched shoes.

"Is the fish still in the tub?" asked the scrivener.

"No," the ferryman replied, "it's already swimming in the river – swimming the way a stone floats."

"Did it make a din?"

"Din enough. It yelled fit to wake the dead and promised me the earth."

The man in the black gown stared into the fire.

"What's to be done with a fish that cries out," he said, not looking at Turlupin, " – a fish that promises one untold wealth in this world and eternal salvation in the next? One should simply toss it back into the water, don't you agree?"

"I've heard tell of such creatures," Turlupin said uneasily, "but I didn't know they really existed."

"Oh yes, there are fish that cry out when their lives are in peril," the man by the fire said in a low voice. "Who truly knows this river, after all? The Seine bargemen, they know it and are privy to its secrets, but they guard such secrets well and are loath to speak of them. And now, my friend, to business."

The pockmarked ferryman took a net from a nail, slung it over his shoulder, and went out. Discounting the pig, which was rooting around in the ashes on the hearth, Turlupin and the scrivener had the hut to themselves.

"Tonight," the scrivener began, "in the house from whose threshold you were so ignominiously dislodged, Pierre de Roncherolles, premier baron of Normandy, is presiding over a conclave attended by representatives of the rebellious nobility from every province in France. It cannot be doubted that they will make decisions inimical to His Majesty the King and the government of the realm. My employer is most anxious to have a confidant in the house of the Lavans – one who will inform him of all that goes on there. I myself cannot enter, my face is too well known."

"Mine too," said Turlupin.

"They saw you only once and will not recognize you – you'll be another person altogether. Listen to this, sir. Fortune has smiled on us. The nobles of Lower Brittany, too, dispatched a delegate to this meeting, one René de Josselin, Sieur de Coetquen. While on his way to Paris, this nobleman suffered a mishap: he was recognized. I challenged him, and, to cut a long story short, he lost the game."

"You played a game?" asked Turlupin. "A game for two? Not Toccadilla, by any chance?"

The man beside the fire emitted a spine-chilling bark of laughter and looked up.

"Yes, a game for two, call it what you will. Suffice it to say, he lost everything: his saddle horse, his clothes, his papers – yes, even his sword and his wig. He had nothing left."

The scrivener abandoned his place by the fire and went over to a chest, from which he produced a handsome new suit of clothes, a pair of hose, a cloak, a sword, a pair of riding boots, a plumed hat, and a wig.

"You see?" he pursued. "Here is all you need to transform yourself into Monsieur de Josselin. Believe me, even your own mother would fail to recognize you in that wig."

"Damnation!" cried Turlupin. "Then I'll not wear it."

"No wig?" the scrivener protested. "Impossible! Every man of rank and quality wears a wig in the style of His Majesty the King. You must wear one or you'll ruin everything. See for yourself, the workmanship is excellent."

"That's true," Turlupin conceded. "The man who made it knew his trade."

"Good," said the scrivener, "so you're being sensible. There's more, so listen carefully. While playing this game with Monsieur de Josselin – Toccadilla, was that what you called it? – I managed to win him over to the King's side. Indeed, such was his newfound alacrity and devotion that he informed me of the passwords that were to gain him admittance to the Hôtel Lavan. They're devilish on their guard in there, as you already know, so mark the passwords well. First, they'll ask your name. Well, what is it?"

"Turlupin."

"No, damn it, you haven't understood! Your name is René de Josselin, Sieur de Coetquen, as your papers duly state. You come from the town of Quimper."

"Very well: René de Josselin, Sieur de Coetquen," Turlupin recited.

"In response to the first question they ask, you will reply: 'With my sword.' Your answer to the next question must be: 'With my life.' That's easy enough to remember. The third question you'll answer by crying out: 'God and the Breton nobility!' Memorize those words and the order in which they occur. Once inside the house you'll have won the day. Discoursing with those noblemen will present you with no difficulty whatever. Their conversation is wholly unrefined. It consists of oaths and curses, crude jests and vile obscenities. Can you curse and swear?"

"Can I!" said Turlupin. "I can swear like a tipsy fishwife."

"That will do admirably," said the scrivener. "And if they question you about your instructions, you've received only one: to demonstrate your willingness to be of service to the house of Lavan come what may. Never refer to servants and lackeys as anything but rogues or fools – that's the unmistakeable mark of a nobleman. Your baggage? You left it at the eating-house where you stopped for breakfast. Then there's Madame la Duchesse. One approaches her with two respectful bows and stands before her bareheaded. Be sure to make no mistake in such matters."

"Bareheaded," Turlupin muttered to himself, "with two respectful bows. It's as well I should know that."

"And now, sir, it'll soon be midnight. Here are your clothes and papers. You'll find me on the river bank tomorrow morning – I'll be waiting for you at the foot of the embankment."

"One more thing," said Turlupin. "This Monsieur de Josselin – he must surely have lost his purse to you as well. I haven't a sou."

"Money?" exclaimed the scrivener. "No, I'll give you no money. A nobleman needs none – he gets others to pay his debts."

It was a quarter past midnight when Turlupin knocked on the door of the Hôtel Lavan. He heard voices, footsteps, and a rattle of keys. Then the door opened a crack, and someone shone a lantern on his plumed hat. The light travelled down him to the toes of his riding boots.

"Your name?"

"René de Josselin, Sieur de Coetquen."

"How do you propose to serve Madame la Duchesse?"

"With my sword."

"And if you lose it?"

"With my life."

"Who instructed you to that effect?"

"God and the Breton nobility!" cried Turlupin.

The door creaked open, and he made his way into a brightly-lit hall flanked by two rows of footmen in black and violet livery. Dazzled by the glare, he shut his eyes.

"We've been expecting you, sir," called a high-pitched, youthful voice. "I bid you welcome to this house."

From his place on the steps, the young Duc de Lavan doffed his hat to Turlupin with a sweeping gesture.

[12]

AT THE SAME hour, the square between the slaughterhouse and the church of Saint-Jacques de la Bougerie was filled with a vast, silent crowd. Criers, porters, discharged lackeys, publicans, coopers, beggars, thieves, carters, bargemen, clerks bereft of work and bread, rag-pickers, water-carriers, fairground singers, hollow-eyed creatures who lived on oatmeal cakes and bran, despairing wretches who combed the vegetable markets for garbage, day labourers, janitors, rowdies, cutpurses, outlaws and fugitives who dared not leave their cellars before dark – all stood wrapped in their rain-sodden coats, waiting for the man who owned them body and soul.

They had come in obedience to an order relayed from street to street and house to house. Undeterred by the rain, they stood there in dogged silence, and so absolute was the hush that reigned over this nocturnal gathering that one could hear the splash of water as it spurted from a Triton's spiral horn into a big stone shell in the middle of the square.

Linkmen hurried by, singly or in little groups, the light from their torches flitting now over the abattoir's massive walls, now over the stone breastwork of the church's portal and its four red granite columns. From far away came the rumble of a passing wagon. Heavy rain clouds pursued their slow, menacing progress across the starless sky.

All at once, the silence of the night was rent by a spine-chilling cry of mingled exultation and lamentation. A man near the Triton fountain had fallen to the ground in a twitching, writhing heap.

"He's here!" he screamed. "He has come, he's among us! I can feel his fire in my heart, his hammerblows in my breast! Here I am, do with me as you will!"

Almost at the same moment, a great cry went up from the portal of the church:

"Monsieur de Saint-Chéron!"

There was a crescendo of excited murmurs and whispers, and the crowd abruptly began to stir. The torches that had converged on the raving visionary scattered, streamed across the square, disappeared from view, and reassembled beneath the portal, which seemed suddenly bathed in the light of day.

Monsieur Gaspard emerged from behind a human wall composed of gigantic figures, his bodyguard of Seine bargemen, and mounted the stone breastwork. The torchlight clearly revealed his furrowed brow and the hollow cheeks that burned with the crimson stigmata of an early death.

He raised one arm. Instantly, the murmurs and whispers died away, and all that could be heard throughout the spacious square was the gentle plashing of the fountain.

Then his words swept across the silent throng.

"The day has come, so hold yourselves in readiness. Justice bids you rise, take up arms, and quit your wretched hovels, your cold hearths. When the hour of the grand shuttlecock tournament strikes, let the drums beat. Rouse the city, haul out the chains, barricade the streets, and end your ills by force of arms. He alone will be punishable who practises moderation, for he that spares an enemy condemns himself. God has delivered them into our hands. We must destroy them all, we must spare not a one, neither man nor woman, old nor young, good nor evil, lest any of them be left alive – lest the memory of their names fail to perish with them."

[13]

"We've yet to begin our deliberations," the Duc de Lavan told Turlupin as they climbed the broad marble staircase. "The outlawed nobility of France has still to be fully represented among those assembled here, and we're all agreed that nothing of consequence may be discussed until the envoy from the house of Vendôme arrives. I await him with impatience. For today, we've confined ourselves to settling a quarrel between Monsieur de la Roche-Pichemer and my cousin Luynes. It was a most tiresome business and exercised us a great deal, for Monsieur de Luynes, being a duke and a peer of the realm, is exempt from fighting duels, and, where Monsieur de la Roche-Pichemer is concerned, there's nothing that could entitle him to –"

He broke off in mid sentence to acknowledge the salute of a nobleman whose grim, dyspeptic face had appeared at a window in the gallery.

"It's he," the young duke whispered, " – Monsieur de la Roche-Pichemer, the very man of whom I was speaking. Devil take it, one can't be too careful. One has only to mention his name, and there he is."

Smiling amiably, Lavan waved once more to the said nobleman, who withdrew into the shadows. Then he turned back to Turlupin.

"And now to you, sir. You come from Brittany. I confess myself eager to learn what instructions you have received from your friends."

"I have but one," said Turlupin, "and that is, to demonstrate my willingness to serve you come what may."

Highly delighted to have memorized the scrivener's words so well, Turlupin looked up at the painted ceiling, which showed Aurora traversing pink clouds in a golden chariot and strewing flowers as she went.

"Well said, sir!" cried the young duke. "There speaks a valiant man. I shall hasten to acquaint Madame with your noble intentions, which do credit both to you and to my house. Are you already lodged, sir? This city is no easy place in which to find good service and decent fare. Landlords are second only to ministers of finance when it comes to robbing people."

"Very true," said Turlupin, who was determined not to leave the house it had cost him so much trouble to enter.

"Why not do me the honour of lodging under my roof?" the duke suggested. "It would be a pleasure, so indulge me in this little matter." Turning, he called, "Maître Hilaire!"

The steward, who had hitherto preserved a respectful distance, came hurrying up.

"Monsieur de Josselin has graciously consented to be my guest," the duke told him. "He's to have a room in the west wing, and see to it that there's a good fire burning. The Saturn or Circe Room will do, or the one with the Sirens."

Turlupin, mindful of his chilly bed at the Widow Sabot's, gave a contented nod when he heard a fire mentioned. Only one thing displeased him, and that was the prospect of sharing a room with other people, the Sirens, for instance. He would sooner have had one to himself.

"I sleep devilish lightly," he said. "It needs only one of those folk to make the slightest noise, the faintest snore, and it'll wake me at once."

"Your Excellency will have no cause for complaint on that

score," the steward hurriedly assured him. "The rooms are quietly situated. The stables and coach-houses are on the other side of the house. Where is Your Excellency's baggage?"

"My baggage? I left it at the eating-house where I stopped for breakfast," said Turlupin, just as the scrivener had impressed on him in the ferryman's hut, but he improvised a few additional words of his own:

"I shall send a couple of rascally servants to fetch it in due course."

The steward withdrew. Turlupin deemed it time to raise the subject that accounted for his presence.

"Where is Madame?" he asked the duke without more ado.

"Madame? She has already retired. It's too late to pay your respects tonight, sir. She spent the day praying with the nuns of the abbey of Port-Royal des Champs. As you must know, sir, the death of the duke, my father, has plunged us into deepest mourning, but we derive some consolation from the thought that his soul, weary of the vain exertions of this life, has attained its true repose."

For a while the young Duc de Lavan stood silent, plunged in thought. Then, with a swift but graceful movement of the head, he readdressed himself to Turlupin.

"I shall now have the honour, sir, of presenting you to Mademoiselle de Lavan, my sister. She will be delighted, I know, to make the acquaintance of so congenial a person. You will find her with some friends of mine, who are being good enough to keep her company."

[14]

FAINTLY UNEASY BUT firmly resolved to show himself a nobleman in each and every respect, Turlupin accompanied the Duc de Lavan into a room whose walls depicted a bewildering abundance of mythological figures: King Cepheus and his royal household, Andromeda chained to her rock at the sea monster's mercy, and Perseus descending from the clouds to rescue her. The niches were occupied by marble statues of amorous couples, shepherds and shepherdesses clasped in each other's arms. Mademoiselle de Lavan, a slender, dainty girl of fifteen, was half reclining in an armchair. Before her, leaning against a table, stood two gallants of whom one held a Bolognese lute. In the background, lost in thought, Monsieur de la Roche-Pichemer sat perched on an andiron, gazing grimly into the firelight, which cast a reddish glow over his yellow satin coat.

"Cléonice," said the Duc de Lavan, "I bring you Monsieur de Josselin, Sieur de Coetquen, a nobleman from the town of Quimper. He arrived in Paris only this morning and is most eager to make your acquaintance. Favour him with your friendship – he's deserving of it."

"Come closer, sir," said the girl. "I'm delighted to see you."

With innumerable bows and vigorous flourishes of his hat, Turlupin stepped out into the middle of the room.

The girl turned to the two gallants. "Thyrsis, Cérilas," she said, "offer Monsieur de Josselin a chair. Quimper? I've never heard of the place. Pardon my ignorance, but where is this Quimper of yours?"

Turlupin was in something of a predicament. He had no idea whether Quimper was situated on a river, in the mountains, or beside the sea – the scrivener had said nothing on the subject. He extricated himself as well as he could.

"Quimper," he said, "is a very sizeable little town, and stands amid the countryside surrounding it."

"Amid the countryside surrounding it," exclaimed the girl. "What a memorable phrase! I like it, upon my soul. Bring me some paper, that I may note it down. 'Quimper stands amid the countryside surrounding it.' Did you hear that, Cérilas?"

"Such precision immediately stamps its author as a man of wit and intellect," said the young nobleman.

Meanwhile, the Duc de Lavan completed his introductions.

"Monsieur de la Roche-Pichemer, Monsieur d'Hunauldaye, Monsieur de Saint-Aignan. Monsieur de Saint-Aignan's name will doubtless be familiar to you. He wrote *Dido,* a tragedy in verse composed pursuant to the rules of the Academy. It was performed at the Louvre last year, on the occasion of Her Majesty's birthday."

"Your humble servant, sir," said Turlupin, with the ready courtesy to which his trade had accustomed him."Mademoiselle, I'm entirely at your service. Sir, my most sincere and heartfelt devotion."

Looking around, he caught a first glimpse of Monsieur de la Roche-Pichemer, who was still sitting apart from the others, and hastened to pay his respects in that quarter too.

"Delighted to make your acquaintance," he told La Roche-Pichemer. "It gives me great pleasure to inform you – "

He broke off in confusion and began to back toward the door, having just recognized Monsieur de la Roche-Pichemer as the nobleman whose horse had kicked the one-legged beggar to death on the Pont-Rouge.

"The pleasure," La Roche-Pichemer drawled indifferently, never taking his eyes off the fire, "– the pleasure, sir, is all mine."

Reassured by his tone, Turlupin breathed a sigh of relief. He had been afraid that La Roche-Pichemer would recognize him as the journeyman barber who had stood on the Pont-Rouge in a threadbare coat and patched shoes, cabbage and razors in hand.

"Join us, sir," Monsieur d'Hunauldaye called from his place at the table. "Do us the honour. Here is wine, here are quinces and pickled peaches. Pray try this almond cake."

On finding himself ignored by Monsieur de la Roche-Pichemer and liberally regaled by the others, Turlupin recovered his composure. Truly, the scrivener had been right: with a wig on his head and a sword at his side, he had become another person altogether.

He raised his glass and drained it to the health of Mademoiselle de Lavan before sitting down at the table.

"This wine," he declared, "is the best I ever drank."

"One perceives you to be a connoisseur," said Monsieur d'Hunauldaye.

Thus emboldened, Turlupin went one better. "It's a truly excellent drop of wine, by all the Turks and Moors!"

"Oh!" exclaimed Mademoiselle de Lavan. "Spare your friends the Turks and Moors, Monsieur de Josselin. One doesn't swear by such uncouth and insensate creatures, one swears by the graceful attributes of Mother Nature: by the blue of the sky, by the zephyr's gentle whisper, by the dance of the Oreads, by Hesperia's gently rolling meadows, by . . . Continue, Thysis!"

"By the desire your lips awaken in me, Cléonice!" Monsieur de Saint-Aignan began."By all the sighs I've devoted to my love, by the ocean than envies the blue of your eyes, by the flames of passion –"

"Enough, Thyrsis! Be silent!" the girl commanded with a most ungracious expression. "That wasn't good. Passion? Ugh! Nothing could be uglier."

"Too true," Turlupin chimed in. "Nothing's more apt to induce smallpox than agitation."

"That's news to me," said Monsieur d'Hunauldaye.

"I had it from a book called *The Seal of Wisdom,*" Turlupin told him in a confidential tone. "It contains some very useful information, among other things, that the finest pomade can be extracted from sheep's feet."

"Sheep's feet, eh?" said Monsieur d'Hunauldaye. "His Majesty the King should be told. He often devotes hours to the preparation of pomades of all kinds."

Turlupin, who had raised his goblet, was so surprised that he forgot to drink.

"Pomades?" he exclaimed. "You mean the king prepares them with his very own hands while his rascally servants look on in idleness?"

"Our great King Louis is a master of many trades," the young nobleman informed him. "He makes rope, nets and saddles, he preserves jam, and in spring he grows peas. He's also a most proficient barber. All the officers of his household have been shaved by him."

"A barber?" yelped Turlupin, staring at Monsieur d'Hunauldaye open-mouthed. "No, that's impossible – it can't be true. I've never seen a barber's tin shaving bowl displayed above the gate of the Louvre."

"His Majesty enjoys it."

Turlupin deposited his glass on the table. "I don't understand," he said, shaking his head. "I find barbering the most irksome of trades, and besides, there's a great injustice here. How can any barber hope to make a modest living if folk go to the king to have their beards shaved off. And you say he enjoys it? Just fancy! Well, I never!"

"Thyrsis," cried Mademoiselle de Lavan, "you sit here plunged in sublime melancholy. I grant you permission to express your feelings in well-turned verses."

"I'd never have thought it," muttered Turlupin, still struggling to regain his composure.

"You have only to command me, Cléonice," said Monsieur de Saint-Aignan.

He seated himself on a stool at the girl's feet, directed a rapturous gaze at the panelled ceiling, and, accompanying his verses on the lute, began to sing in a very melodious voice:

"When still thy love was mine alone,
o shepherdess with golden hair,
when still thy gaze held me in thrall – "

"Does he make wigs too?" asked Turlupin.

"– I felt a joy beyond compare.
All manner of endearments sweet
thy lips bestowed upon my ear.
For ever will my heart preserve – "

"The King," Turlupin persisted, " – does he really shave folk's chins? It passes my understanding."

"– those memories of yesteryear.
That, then, is why I sing my songs
in praise of her whom I love best – "

"Enough!" cried Mademoiselle de Lavan. "Your verses, Thyrsis, are truly indifferent today. I've heard lovers do a great deal better."

Having coaxed some mournful minor chords from his instrument, Monsieur de Saint-Aignan obediently brought his song to an end:

"My lute I now must lay aside,
o shepherdess, at thy behest."

He rose with a sorrowful air, sighed deeply, and bowed.

"You're being very cruel, Cléonice, to the most faithful of your friends. You know that I love you."

"I know it," said the girl, flicking some little pellets of bread at Andromeda's bosom. "I know it, but I've never attached any importance to your feelings."

"Speaking for myself," said Turlupin, "I found it most noteworthy, what was sung by this gentleman whose name escapes me. I regret never having learned to play such an instrument and sing to it."

"Before you arrived on the scene, sir," the luckless lutenist told him, "I still nursed a modicum of hope. Now, however, I must fear the worst. Cléonice loves you, of that there's no doubt. Won't you say a word in my favour? I appeal to your goodness of heart."

Turlupin gave the young nobleman a friendly pat on the shoulder.

"I understand little of these matters," he said, "but of one thing I'm certain: Mademoiselle is one of those persons with whom a suitor must always start afresh. Don't be put out. My advice is, try presenting her with little gifts – flowers one day, ribbons or gloves or a flask of perfume the next."

"By heaven," exclaimed Monsieur d'Hunauldaye, "that's not a bad notion. What do you think of it, Cléonice?"

"I think," said the girl, tapping Turlupin's wig with her fan, "that Monsieur de Josselin is thoroughly impertinent, but many allowances must be made for a nobleman who hails from so far afield. I find him charming. Monsieur de Josselin, I know that you love me, and I grant you permission to tell me so."

"Have pity on me, Cléonice!" wailed Monsieur de Saint-Aignan. "You're killing me. Your every word transfixes my heart."

Monsieur de la Roche-Pichemer rose from his place beside the hearth. He stood there with his arms crossed and a look of bitter contempt on his face, which was bathed in the glow from the fire.

"Such is the lover of today!" he said scornfully. "He dons a tragic mask, he sighs, he addresses the beloved with tears in his eyes, he swoons if she scolds him for an instant. What a foolish age we live in! Our forefathers despised sentimental speeches and languishing sighs, but they found their sweethearts no less ready to join them in the Dance of Toulouse."

Mademoiselle de Lavan gave a horrified, indignant little scream and clapped her hands over her ears.

"Shame on you! Shame on you, Monsieur de la Roche-Pichemer! How dare you speak of such things in my presence!"

"The Dance of Toulouse," Turlupin repeated thoughtfully. "Your pardon, but I'm unfamiliar with that measure."

"The Dance of Toulouse," Monsieur d'Hunauldaye explained, "is the name we give to a diverting game for two from which victor and vanquished derive equal pleasure."

"Cérilas," Mademoiselle de Lavan exclaimed delightedly, "I congratulate you. You have just devised the most elegant words possible to describe a gross, beastly, vulgar activity."

"*Now* I know the game you mean," said Turlupin. "But we call it Toccadilla. I often look on while our vicar plays it with one of my oafish servants."

"What!" cried Monsieur d'Hunauldaye. "Did I hear you aright? Your vicar plays it with one of your servants – in the Italian manner, too? How droll!"

"And the best of it is," gurgled Mademoiselle de Lavan, shaking with laughter, " – the best of it is, this worthy priest allows Monsieur de Josselin to watch him at it. Just imagine! The diversions of country life are surely second to none!"

Turlupin was annoyed to note that he had become an object of amusement. The reason for this general hilarity escaped him.

"I don't know what's so amusing," he said with a reproachful glance at Mademoiselle de Lavan. "I see nothing to laugh at.

Toccadilla is an entertaining little pastime, that's all. As for you, sir," he went on, turning to Monsieur de la Roche-Pichemer, whose mocking, supercilious smile exasperated him most of all, "– as for you, there's nothing, as I'm very well aware, that could entitle you to – "

"Well?"said La Roche-Pichemer, and the smile vanished from his face."I'm listening and waiting, sir. What is it you have to tell me?"

"Nothing more," Turlupin replied, for that was as far as the Duc de Lavan had got. "Nothing more. That's all I wished to say."

Monsieur de la Roche-Pichemer sauntered up to Turlupin, came to a halt, and eyed him closely. All at once, it dawned on Turlupin that what confronted him in the person of this nobleman was disaster, ruination, and the end of his venture.

Silence had fallen on all sides.

"The longer I reflect on the matter," La Roche-Pichemer said abruptly, "the more certain I feel that this is not our first encounter. No, I'm not mistaken: I've seen you before."

Turlupin turned deathly pale and his throat tightened with fear, but he didn't give himself away. He summoned up all his strength, determined to prove himself a nobleman at this crucial juncture.

"I remember you very well," La Roche-Pichemer went on. "I don't know where it was or when, but I haven't forgotten your face. You were standing but two paces distant, staring at me in such a manner that I was tempted to have you thrashed by my lackeys."

Turlupin drew himself up. No reference having been made to his cabbage, razors and patched shoes, his courage revived.

"I see," he said firmly. "I'm glad you told me. So you had a mind to have me thrashed by your lackeys. Well and good, but believe me, they would have tackled the wrong man. What's more, were I not constrained by my regard for Monsieur le Duc de Lavan, who has the honour to be my host – "

La Roche-Pichemer gestured to indicate that he had a proposal to make.

"I fully understand your wish for satisfaction," he said casually. "Well, far be it from me to deprive you of it. May I hazard a small suggestion, sir? There is, in the garden, a pretty little stretch of sand. You'll find it if you take fifty paces to your front from the left-hand postern and then turn right. If you're agreeable, I shall await you there with a friend at nightfall tomorrow."

"Excellent," Turlupin replied, highly gratified that La Roche-Pichemer took him for a nobleman. While speaking, he was reminded of the words he'd heard the Picard nobleman utter in Madame Sabot's barbershop two days before. They seemed admirably suited to the occasion.

"A duel by torchlight, eh?" he remarked. "Capital. This promises to be amusing."

He favoured Monsieur de la Roche-Pichemer with an inclination of the head, then bowed to the others.

"Mademoiselle, pray regard me as your humble servant. Gentlemen, be assured of my profound respect. I have the honour to bid you all adieu."

"I forbid you," cried Mademoiselle de Lavan, when Turlupin had left the room, " – I simply forbid you to duel with Monsieur de Josselin. You insulted him. You will extend your apologies."

Monsieur de la Roche-Pichemer tossed a log on the fire and resumed his seat astride the andiron.

"Mademoiselle," he replied, "the power you exercise over me is not, thank God, unlimited. I shall fight your peculiar nobleman, and that's that."

"But I don't wish you to! I forbid it. He's witty, whimsical, amusing. He pleases me."

"He pleases you? Well, he doesn't please me," La Roche-Pichemer retorted with a shrug. "'Monsieur le Duc de Lavan, who has the honour to be my host . . . 'Is *that* witty? Do you find *that* amusing? Besides – can it really have escaped you? – he reeks of onions! That does nothing to endear him to me, either."

[15]

TURLUPIN HAD TAKEN refuge in a dark corner of the gallery. He stood there a prey to the fear of death, his distracted soul torn between rage and despair.

"Why in the world should that nobleman be so hell-bent on skewering me with his sword?" he asked himself for the hundredth time. "What in God's name are these folk, Christians or heathens? He'll run me through a few times and leave me dead on the sand. Where's his religion? It shouldn't be allowed. Who'd have thought it possible? I've landed myself in a fine mess, and no mistake."

Goaded by fear and disquiet, he began to pace up and down.

"It's dangerous, being a nobleman," he whispered. "You eat, you drink, you make merry, and before you know it you're lying on the sand with so many sword-thrusts in your body that no surgeon can set you on your feet again. The damned scoundrel laughed in my face! Him and his yellow satin suit! I'll teach the miserable blackguard – I won't make it easy for him to kill me. He'll get his share!"

In the barbershop not long ago, Monsieur Le Gouche had shown the landlord of the Taverne des Apôtres how to adopt the quarte and the tierce and how to lunge. Remembering this, Turlupin withdrew his sword from its scabbard and aimed some furious cuts and thrusts at a white marble Diana kneeling with her spear levelled at some invisible quarry.

But Turlupin's hand was too accustomed to wielding a razor to support the weight of a sword.

"It's no use," he groaned. "Duelling is an exhausting business, and you mustn't remain still for an instant or you're done for. Besides, there are quintes and feints and secondes and parades and charades, and those I failed to note. I should have paid more heed, but now it's too late. If only I were allowed to fight him with my fists, I'd pin him against a wall and squeeze till he yielded oil, but swordplay? No, it's hopeless."

Tired out, he stood staring into the shadows with the naked blade in his hand.

"What if I land a blow before he manages to get his sword out of the scabbard? What if I lunge at him without shouting 'On guard!'? One, two, and it's all over – I doff my hat and go my way. But that's no use, either, God knows. You have to wait for the signal – Monsieur Le Gouche said so. You can't simply start when you choose. There's a whole host of formalities to be completed before you're permitted to attack."

But no sooner had he dismissed the possibility of saving his skin in this way than another idea occurred to him – one that seemed easier of execution and far more sensible.

"This house is swarming with noblemen versed in swordplay," he told himself. "What if I could persuade one of them to duel in my place with that spiteful, irascible fool of an aristocrat? I'll have a word with the duke, who gave me such a friendly, hospitable welcome. He shows every sign of knowing how to wield a sword. Perhaps he'll do me this favour if I ask it of him. Upon my soul, I'd sooner see him lying dead on the sand than myself."

So saying, he sheathed his blade and went in search of the Duc de Lavan.

Young Lavan was standing in a window recess in the great banqueting hall with Pierre de Roncherolles, doyen of the

Norman nobility, a tall, handsome old man of imposing aspect. They were discussing the means to be employed in persuading the Duc d'Enghien, son of Monsieur le Prince, to side with the disaffected nobility. From the banqueting table that ran along the right-hand wall came the clink of glasses and the sound of merry laughter. Seated there, boisterously drinking and arguing, were three noblemen who, though strangers until today, had already sealed their friendship with wine. Monsieur Le Coqu-Corbeille, Baron de Lavedan, a corpulent man of thoughtful disposition, had come to Paris from the district of Saintonge. Never having seen the city before, he was thoroughly bemused by the multitude of coaches and carriages that had passed him in the streets. Facing him sat Graf von Mömpelgard, a German count deputed to attend this meeting by the nobility of Lorraine. Mömpelgard was a brawler, gambler and drinker, quick-tempered and immensely strong but gentle as a lamb when tipsy. He had come accompanied by one of his hounds, which lay asleep at his feet. The third man at the table was Monsieur de Caille et de Rougon, captain of the Royal Navarra Regiment, a dashing blade, feared and loved, bold and impulsive. Rumour had it that, when a lady called on him to collect a debt one morning while he was still abed, he politely escorted her to the door in a state of utter nakedness.

Graf von Mömpelgard had just begun to speak when Turlupin appeared in the doorway and bowed low. He was lolling back in his chair with his sword across his thighs and a goblet of wine in his hand.

"We nobles of Lorraine," he boomed, "are honourable men, and noble by nature as well as name. My three sons, my five brothers, my cousins – "

"Your servant, sirs," said Turlupin, finding himself ignored. He bowed low a second time.

"My cousins, my neighbours and friends," Graf von Mömpelgard pursued, "– all of them, when their courage and loyalty are in demand, take up arms and muster to the sound of drum, fife and cymbal. Such is the custom in Lorraine."

"Your most humble servant at all times," said Turlupin, and performed a third bow.

"Monsieur de Josselin!" called the young duke, who had at last caught sight of him. "It delights me see you. I'd been craving your presence, upon my honour."

"I'm not in favour of drums and fifes," said Monsieur Le Coqu-Corbeille. "We must set to work cautiously and prudently, with logic and deliberation, step by step. We must begin by inciting the Grand Council against the Cardinal, and the Parliaments against the Grand Council, and the common folk against the audit offices and courts of assize. Such is my plan, and I think it a good one. The common folk must declare for us and take our side. Then we can proceed to transform the Cardinal's authority into an object of universal disregard."

"Capital!" cried Graf von Mömpelgard. "An object of universal disregard! Well said!"

"Yes, but all must be done by degrees. One thing at a time – no commotion, no undue haste, no fifes and cymbals."

"Monsieur de Roncherolles," the young duke said deferentially to the old man at his side, "permit me to commend to your attention Monsieur de Josselin, Sieur de Coetquen, a Breton nobleman desirous of paying his respects to the venerable Anchises of the Norman nobility."

"Your lordship's most humble and devoted servant," Turlupin declared with a sweep of the hand that might have signalled his readiness, not only to trim the old nobleman's beard but also to curl his hair on the spot.

Unhappily, his respectful words were drowned by a furious outburst on the part of Monsieur de Caille et de Rougon.

"Caution, prudence, deliberation!" he bellowed, thumping the table until the glasses rattled. "Those words are fit for filling the ears but naught else – they're pitchers with nothing in 'em, dishes with nothing on 'em! If that's your plan, sir, I'd as soon have left my sword hanging on its hook."

He rose and leaned forward with both fists propped on the table, his face empurpled with wine and vehemence.

"Let me tell you, sir, what a lifetime's experience has taught me, for I've not spent an unventuresome day since my fifteenth year, and God has never and nowhere denied me my share of dangers. You don't win a war with petty plots and machinations, sir: you win it with your backside in the saddle!"

"Capital!" exclaimed Graf von Mömpelgard. "With your backside in the saddle . . . By the horned devil and the souls of the damned, that's the only way to win a war!"

"And that's what I call an oath," said Turlupin, filled with admiration.

"But we haven't remained awake to hatch plans and squabble," the German nobleman pursued. "We've remained awake for the sake of friendship, good cheer and good wine, so drink up!"

He raised his goblet and drained it, then lolled back in his chair and proceeded to sing in a sonorous bass, beating time with his fists. He sang of the pious beggar on Toulouse Bridge, who shared his crumbs of bread with the fish in the Garonne:

"Across the bridge my way I hied,
– one must, to reach Toulouse –
and there a beggar I espied
who smelled not like a rose."

"There's a great deal of sense in that song," Turlupin remarked to the Duc de Lavan, " – the one being sung by the gentleman with silver buttons on his sleeves. It's very true, as I myself can confirm: those villainous beggars make a habit of standing on bridges or in narrow alleyways, so that everyone has to brush past them."

Meantime, Mömpelgard sang on:

> *"He did not smell of rosemary,*
> *nor yet of mignonette.*
> *His cap he then held out to me – "*

"Rosemary, mignonette?" Turlupin exclaimed. "I should think not! Beggars reek of horse dung and filth, of pestilence and turnips rotting in the gutter. It's indescribable, what they smell of at times. I'm surprised they're permitted to walk the streets."

"One can tell you arrived in Paris only this morning," said the Duc de Lavan. "You're still unaccustomed to the sight of those unfortunate creatures. But tell us, Monsieur de Josselin, how did you spend the day?"

Turlupin stared at the duke, wide-eyed with alarm. He was wholly unprepared for such a question, never having given any thought to how a nobleman would pass the time in Paris. And then, in his predicament, he remembered the sarcastic words with which he had been greeted the previous day by Monsieur Pigeot, the dyer, and promptly made use of them.

"Well now," he said, "one knows how to while away the time. One goes for a stroll, one greets one's friends, one prattles and gossips."

Becoming bolder, he added:

"In the afternoon I paid a call on a young woman. Her husband returned unexpectedly, so I had to retire to the attic. I spent several hours among bundles of thatch, with only a cat for company."

"Take care, by thunder!" cried Graf von Mömpelgard. "One must never mention those animals in the presence of a hound.

It's lucky he's asleep and failed to hear you, or he'd have flown at your throat."

Turlupin hastened to make good his mistake.

"I had no idea he dislikes one to speak of cats," he said with a timid glance at the huge beast, "or I should never have uttered the word. I dislike cats too. Damnation, now he's awake! Hold him, sir – hold him fast! It wasn't a cat, tell him – it was a rat."

The hound raised its head, gave a brief, menacing growl, and bared its teeth. The German nobleman cursed like a madman and Turlupin took refuge behind the Duc de Lavan.

"He'd better not try to attack me," he said, but far from loudly. "I'll throttle him – I'll break every bone in his body."

Taking the duke by the arm, Turlupin drew him into a distant corner of the room and addressed him in a low, persuasive tone.

"As you know, sir," he said, "no one could take a keener interest than I in all that concerns you. Well, one of the three noblemen I first encountered here – I forget his name, but he wears a suit of yellow satin and a wig in the style known as *cadinette* or *à la Mirleton*, parted in the centre with the hair hanging down in long ringlets on either side – he was seated by the fire –"

"Monsieur de la Roche-Pichemer?"

"The same – yes, that was his name. Well, he dislikes you, does Monsieur de la Roche-Pichemer."

"I'm aware of that," said the Duc de Lavan, "but I don't account him a friend of mine either."

"He spoke of you in a manner that enraged me," Turlupin went on. "He intimated – no, he insinuated – that he respects you less than any man on earth."

"What!" the duke exclaimed. "Did he really dare to say such a thing?"

"I've never deceived anyone in my life," Turlupin assured him, "and God forbid that you should be the first. There's nothing for it: you must fight him. Honour demands it."

"Honour may demand it," the duke said thoughtfully, "but politics and common sense forbid me to cross swords with a member of Monsieur d'Enghien's circle. That most celebrated prince, whom we're anxious to enlist on behalf of our cause, regards Monsieur de la Roche-Pichemer as a bosom friend. Now do you understand why I, for my part, must do my utmost to persuade Monsieur de la Roche-Pichemer to forget the treatment he received today at the hands of my cousin Luynes?"

"So you won't fight him?" Turlupin asked gloomily.

The duke's sole response was a shrug. Turlupin stared at the floor. His situation was desperate. He felt he had been forsaken, ignominiously and on the flimsiest of pretexts, by one whose friendship he had taken for granted. He began to hate this youth who had abandoned him to his fate with bland, urbane words and a shrug of the shoulders.

"To tell the truth," the duke continued after a while, "I've never understood their friendship. No one in the kingdom stands higher than Monsieur d'Enghien, whereas Monsieur de la Roche-Pichemer is a penurious younger son. He owns next to nothing, not even the lieutenant's commission he holds in some regiment or other, I forget which. That he purchased with money advanced him by Madame d'Orseigne, the wife of a Châtelet attorney, who was his mistress for a spell."

Turlupin looked up, his eyes ablaze with rage, malice, and wild, triumphant elation.

"So he's a younger son, this Monsieur de la Roche-Pichemer," he said tensely, " – that's why he owns nothing. His elder brother owns everything, I suppose: country seat, town house, horses, carriages, gold coin?"

The Duc de Lavan nodded. "Yes, in conformity with the right of inheritance and the laws of France."

"You don't say!" Turlupin exulted. "So the elder brother gets everything. That's what I call a sensible arrangement. What of you, sir – what would *you* do if *you* were a younger son? What if someone turned up who could prove he was your elder brother and satisfy Parliament to that effect – what would you do then, sir?"

The Duc de Lavan threw back his head and laughed.

"I?" he said. "I'd buy me a mule and a handbell and peddle my old plumed hats through the streets of Paris." He assumed the voice and manner of a street vendor. "Plumed hats! Who'll buy my plumed hats? Hither to me, all who wish to buy a plumed hat!"

Turlupin shook his head.

"I wouldn't advise it," he said. "That trade won't earn you much. Common folk don't buy plumed hats, they wear the old rabbitskin caps they're accustomed to. The mule and the handbell would be a waste of money."

"You're very droll," said the Duc de Lavan, baffled by the Breton nobleman's bizarre remarks.

[16]

CONVERSATION AT THE table had become still livelier and noisier. Monsieur Le Coqu-Corbeille doffed his hat, drew his sword, and drank the king's health. Graf von Mömpelgard tried to wrest the blade from his hand and preached peace and reconciliation. Monsieur de Caille et de Rougon inveighed against the nobility of Provence, who had declined to send a representative to the meeting.

"Those Provençaux," he bellowed, "they think they have a monopoly of the world's intelligence. Any fire's too hot for them and any water too deep. They prefer to watch and wait – they side with whichever party gains the upper hand."

"Judas has many kinfolk in those parts," said Monsieur Le Coqu-Corbeille.

Graf von Mömpelgard drained his glass with an air of deepest melancholy.

"I've said it before," he lamented. "There'll be war again, and it won't spare Lorraine, God's green garden, land of oakwoods and vine-covered hills. No one believes me, but war will come and bear us all away with it: my sons, my beloved cousins, my friends – "

"*Volentem ducit, nolentem trahit,*" said Monsieur de Roncherolles, who was standing apart in the shadowy window bay. "That applies to wine, war, and the Christian faith."

"Admirably put, upon my honour," exclaimed Monsieur de Caille et de Rougon. "I say that quite frankly, gentlemen, though I never studied Latin because wax candles were dear in my boyhood and my father was a frugal man. 'Aspire to valour,' he told me, ' – you're fit for nothing else.' He did me an injustice in not permitting me to study Latin, for scholars are esteemed more highly than soldiers in this godforsaken age. Thirty-seven years I've served my king. He has made me rich in fine words, but my purse is empty."

"He makes everyone rich in fine words," said Graf von Mömpelgard.

"Damned to hell be anyone who denies His Majesty due respect!" cried Monsieur Le Coqu-Corbeille, brandishing his sword in his right hand and his goblet in his left. "I'm ready and willing to cross swords with any man who speaks ill of His Majesty."

Turlupin pricked up his ears. Here was a nobleman who had declared himself ready to cross swords with all comers, and the naked blade lent him with a very warlike appearance. Turlupin drew nearer.

"If that's your wish," he said, "I've something to tell you. There is beneath this roof a nobleman who had the effrontery to speak of His Majesty the King in a most disrespectful manner."

"Really? He dared to do that? What did he say, this nobleman?"

"He said that His Majesty the King takes pleasure in shaving his officers with his own hand. He further stated that he esteemed His Sanctified Majesty no more highly than a razor, a cupping glass, a pair of scissors, a sponge – "

"Hell's bells and buckets of blood!" cried Monsieur Le Coqu-Corbeille. "He said that in your hearing? I sincerely hope, sir, that you chastised him on the spot as he deserved."

Alarmed to note that the nobleman's ire was directed more against himself than Monsieur de la Roche-Pichemer, Turlupin fell back on the defensive.

"I challenged him to a duel," he replied miserably.

"You did right," said Monsieur Le Coqu-Corbeille.

"And you, sir," asked Turlupin, "what do you propose to do?"

"I?" the nobleman said with dignity. "I shall congratulate you when you've redeemed the honour of His Majesty the King by killing the fellow."

"Spare him, good sir, spare him!" Graf von Mömpelgard called across the table, rendered meek and peaceable by wine. "He, too, was born of woman. Forgive him, that you yourself may be forgiven."

Turlupin stared moodily into space. Another attempt had misfired. One of these two noblemen was preaching brotherly love, and the other, for all his bold and bellicose utterances, was just as unprepared to fight Monsieur de la Roche-Pichemer in his, Turlupin's, place. He now pinned his hopes on the third nobleman seated at the table, the one whose face bore more than a dozen scars.

Turlupin gave the sleeping hound a wide berth and sidled up to Monsieur de Caille et de Rougon.

"Sir," he began, choosing his words with care, "may I beg the favour of a word with you?"

Monsieur de Caille et de Rougon jumped to his feet with a jingle of spurs. He was so short, he barely came up to Turlupin's shoulder. Finding himself confronted by a nobleman whose face was unfamiliar to him, he bowed in the most ceremonious fashion and swept off his hat.

"I do not know if I have had the honour of being introduced to you," he said. "I am Jean Dagobert de Caille et de Rougon, captain in the Royal Navarra Regiment."

He paused in the expectation that Turlupin would state his name, but Turlupin said nothing, merely stared up at the panelled ceiling with a flustered, perplexed expression.

"Your name, sir?" asked the captain.

Turlupin ran a hand over his brow and wig, his face a picture of discomfiture and vexation. The noble name he bore in this house had completely slipped his memory. From the ceiling his eyes travelled downwards to the Venetian mirror that reflected Monsieur Le Coqu-Corbeille's broad, red face, to the candles burning in their silver girandoles, to the wine bottles and glasses, to Graf von Mömpelgard's plumed hat, to the bunches of lace on Monsieur de Caille et de Rougon's scarlet breeches, but he still couldn't recollect his name. All that escaped his lips was an indistinct murmur.

"Your pardon, sir," the captain said, very quietly and courteously, "but I didn't catch your name."

"Granted," Turlupin replied with a grand gesture. "Forgiven and forgotten. 'Nough said."

"Having stated my name, I demand to know yours," the captain said indignantly. "Speak, or I'll compel you to extend the courtesy you decline to show me of your own free will."

And he slapped the hilt of his sword. To his horror, Turlupin realized that he was threatened with two duels instead of one.

"Damnation!" he exclaimed. "The wine's to blame, that's all. Who was it persuaded me to drain so many glasses, one after another? Believe it or not, I can't remember my own name. It's a fact, I've forgotten it. My head's in a whirl. If you were to ask me where I am and whether I'm in Paris, I couldn't tell you that either."

To gloss over the subject as quickly as possible, he essayed a change of tack. Leaning forward, he addressed the captain in a confidential whisper.

"You ought to grow a beard, you know. It sets off the physiognomy."

"Mother of God!" the captain bellowed angrily. "I don't tolerate ridicule. What concern of yours is my physiognomy? Enough of this tomfoolery, sir. Draw!"

But the Duc de Lavan stepped between them just in time.

"Gently, sir, gently!" he urged the captain. "Monsieur de Josselin has a dry sense of humour. He's fond of jesting and says the drollest things with the most earnest expression in the world. He has forgotten his name? Permit me to jog his memory: Monsieur de Josselin, Sieur de Coetquen, envoy of the Breton nobility, a newcomer to Paris from the town of Quimper."

Turlupin cast a grateful glance at the duke.

"Quimper, Josselin, Sieur de Coetquen," he muttered to himself, determined not to forget the words again.

"Monsieur de Josselin?" the captain exclaimed in an entirely different tone of voice. "You mean I have the honour to address the son of the man under whose orders I commanded the infantry in Brittany seven years ago? Pardon my impetuosity, sir. How fares Monsieur le Marquis?"

"Sieur de Coetquen, Josselin, Quimper," muttered Turlupin. "Josselin, Quimper, Sieur de Coetquen." Aloud, he said, "He's very well, heaven be praised."

"I'm delighted to hear it," the captain declared. "It's seven years since I saw him. And how are my cousin the Chevalier and my red-haired friend L'Estoile?"

"They're on good terms," Turlupin replied boldly. "They see each other almost every day."

"What!" cried Monseur de Caille et de Rougon. "They're reconciled, you say? Incredible! And they were mortal enemies. The Chevalier and L'Estoile! To think I should hear it thus!"

"Yes indeed, they're the best of friends," Turlupin assured him. "Your cousin stood sponsor at the christening of L'Estoile's child."

"What did you say?" the captain exclaimed. "Redpoll has a child? He, who never cared for a woman in his life? Whom did he marry, in God's name?"

"His neighbour's niece," Turlupin groaned. "How hot it is in here. I'm stifling."

Monsieur de Caille et de Rougon threw up his hands in boundless amazement and flopped down on his chair.

"Did I hear you aright?" he cried. "He married Mademoiselle de Villarseux, the little hunchback? What a notion! He turned down Monsieur de Joigny's daughter, her and her twenty-five thousand livres a year, and took a fancy to the little hunchback? Well, he always was a fool, and he'll remain one to his dying day. What does Monsieur de Joigny say to that? Yes, what's he up to these days, Monsieur de Joigny?"

Turlupin was in despair. "He's gone into the cloth trade," he said dully.

"The cloth trade?" Monsieur de Caille et de Rougon leapt to his feet again and stared at Turlupin in amazement. "What are you saying? What of his estates, his demesnes, his forests, his houses?"

"He doesn't own them any more," Turlupin said, taking the plunge. "He gambled them all away."

"God in heaven!" cried the captain. "Gambled them away? What a calamity for him and his children! Someone must have swindled the old man. What rogue cheated him out of his possessions in such a manner?"

Unable to think up a suitable name, Turlupin was cornered and he knew it.

"There were several of them," he said hurriedly. "But the old man isn't doing too badly, for all that. He still keeps an excellent table. The last time I dined with him we had *ragoût chasseur* – do you know the dish?"

Without giving the captain time to interpose another question, he went on:

"*Ragoût chasseur* . . . For that you need a piece of veal, a slice of ham, not cut too thin, and a wing of partridge. What else?

Ah yes, an egg for the gravy, vinegar, pepper, butter for braising the sliced meat, mustard, vinegar, pepper – "

Monsieur de Caille et de Rougon tried to stem Turlupin's torrent of words.

"And what does Monsieur de Joigny – "

"Vinegar, mustard, pepper, oil," Turlupin repeated firmly. "Butter for braising the mutton, also chopped onion – "

"Just one more question, sir – "

"Yes indeed, onion too," Turlupin insisted. "Not too much, mark you – no more than a pinch, half an ounce chopped very fine. *Ragoût chasseur* . . . I'm surprised you're unacquainted with the dish. At home in Brittany we – "

"Hush! Silence!" the Duc de Lavan called out. "Listen, what's that outside?"

A babble of voices was coming from the gallery, where lackeys could be heard bustling to and fro. The steward appeared in the doorway.

"The envoy from the house of Vendôme," the duke exclaimed. "Did he give his name?"

"Yes, Excellency: François, Comte de Beaupuis."

"Le Dangereux!" cried the duke. "It's Le Dangereux. He actually dared to enter Paris – what folly!"

"Tell me one more thing, sir," the captain entreated.

"Le Dangereux!" Turlupin cut in. "It's Le Dangereux! I must see him. Au revoir, sir, I must go to him at once. More of your friends another time."

And he hurried off, leaving a pensive Monsieur de Caille et de Rougon to ponder on the changes that had befallen his friends in Brittany.

[17]

FRANÇOIS LE DANGEREUX, Comte de Beaupuis, victor of Lens and Rocroy, Lion of France; Le Dangereux, convicted of lèse-majesté for high treason and a participant in all the anti-government rebellions and conspiracies of recent years; Le Dangereux, whose name appeared in the four articles of the Treaty of Madrid; Le Dangereux, who could not fail to die on the scaffold if he fell into the Cardinal's hands, was standing on the stairs with a silken half-mask in his hand, still wearing the travel-stained apparel in which he had alighted from his horse.

The disaffected nobility of France crowded around to bid him welcome. Proud bearers of France's greatest and most illustrious names – the two Comtes de Broglie, the Ducs de Luynes, de Nevers, de Noirmoutier and de Bouillon, Prince d'Aubijoux from the house of Amboise, Prince de Marsillac from the house of La Rochefoucauld, provincial delegates such as the Vicomte d'Aubeterre of Péronne, the Chevalier de Lansac and Monsieur de Bragelone, both of Poitou, the Chevalier de Frontenac, the plenipotentiary from Champagne, Monsieur de la Magdelaine of Montdidier, Monsieur de Berteauville, elected envoy of the Burgundian nobility, Baron de Saint-Aldegonde of Le Perche – all those whom hatred of the Cardinal had brought to this house flocked to greet his outlawed mortal foe: Le Dangereux, France's most celebrated warrior.

Frenzied enthusiasm had overcome them. Now that they could see in their midst the man whom Richelieu feared more than any other, they were confident that their venture would be crowned with success. That Le Dangereux had defied a death sentence to come to Paris struck them as more than a good omen; to them it seemed an outward and visible sign of the impotence of the regime which they had fought throughout their lives with a loathing inherited from their fathers.

They vented their joy at this stroke of daring in wild and ecstatic cries: "Le Dangereux! It's Le Dangereux! All honour to Monsieur de Vendôme for sending us his best man."

"We had no general. Now that we have one, we must strike!"

"The battle's decided before it has begun!"

"The Lion of France against the Rat of France . . . What a spectacle!"

The jubilant aristocrats were behaving like madmen. Turlupin stood apart, leaning against the balustrade and watching them with indifferent eyes. His anger wasn't aroused until he caught sight of his enemy, Monsieur de la Roche-Pichemer, in the midst of the pandemonium.

"The wretch," he muttered. "That nobleman who just arrived – the one who looks a regular brawler and bully – him he hugs and embraces and treats like a lord of creation. With him he's on good terms, but me he seeks to kill. I suspect he guesses that I've never learned to wield a sword properly, so he thinks I'll be easy meat. Well, he's mistaken, by the blood of Christ! I'll show him a thing or two!"

Turlupin's sudden confidence and eagerness for the fray were attributable to a good idea that had just occurred to him:

"The scrivener – he'll know what to do!" he told himself. "He gave me the right answer to every question in advance, so he's bound to know all manner of dueller's tricks. He'll advise me on how to give that arrogant rogue his just deserts. The blackguard! So he thought it safe to pick a quarrel with me, did he? Well, he was wrong. I'm not alone – I have a friend in need."

Turlupin rubbed his hands together, knowing that he could meet his ally on the river bank at any time. So great was his faith in the scrivener's acumen that he yearned to consult him at once, but the door was locked and he could think of no pretext that might have enabled him to leave the house for a spell at this late hour.

Meanwhile, triumphantly flourishing their hats, sashes and swords, the noblemen were escorting the Duc de Vendôme's envoy upstairs to the banqueting room. Turlupin brought up the rear.

Bottles of wine were opened, candles lit, and toasts drunk to the Duc de Vendôme and his two sons. Monsieur Le Coqu-Corbeille, now thoroughly inebriated, had retired into a corner and was silently, solemnly dancing a pavane to the accompaniment of music audible to himself alone.

Le Dangereux was speaking of Madame de Vendôme in an undertone:

"She has become very odd, Madame la Duchesse, since she embarked on life in exile. She never leaves the house, not even to attend Mass. She maintains a court consisting of a pimp, a monkey, a blackamoor, a lutenist, a clown, and a poodle."

"And Madame de Chevreuse?" inquired the Prince de Marsillac.

"She has lodgings in Mons, a small town near the frontier, and is burning with impatience for a sight of her old friends in Paris."

"Mons, Mons, I know that name," Baron de Saint-Aldegonde said thoughtfully. "Mons . . . Isn't that the town where they manufacture playing cards?"

Monsieur de Caille et de Rougon, flushed with wine, rose from his place at the other end of the table.

"Everyone knows you've made a pact with the Devil, Le Dangereux," he called. "Everyone has known it since the time of Lens and Rocroy and the storming of Les Sables-d'Olonne." He divided his remarks between Le Dangereux and the others. "You laugh? It's true, by the God that created me: he's bulletproof. Show them the infernal breviary you keep up your sleeve! No lead can bite him, no steel transfix him – we saw it for ourselves at Les Sables-d'Olonne. He's in league with the Princes of Hell. But tell me, Le Dangereux, how the devil did you manage to pass unrecognized through so many towns and fortresses on your way to Paris from the Flanders border?"

"There are twenty-four of them," Turlupin told his neighbour, Monsieur de Bragelone, in an awestruck whisper.

"Twenty-four fortresses between Flanders and Paris?" queried the envoy from Poitou, looking puzzled.

"No, twenty-four Princes of Hell," Turlupin informed him. "What's more, I know their names: Lucifer, their chief, Beelzebub, Satan, Amraphel – "

"Nothing could have been easier," said Le Dangereux. "By day I slept at inns – "

"Belial, the quarrelsome devil," Turlupin went on, "Merodachbal, Vahardinur, Asmodeus, the devil of gluttony – "

" – and by night I marched with the Cardinal's troops."

"Behemoth, the devil of bestiality; Asarchadon, the devil of obscenity; Merosochad, Chisuthros – "

"Merciful God, what manner of names are those?" whispered Monsieur de Bragelone, appalled by Turlupin's arcane revelations.

"With the cardinal's troops? What audacity!" exclaimed the Duc de Noirmoutier. "Ah, so the Cardinal's mustering troops, is he?"

"I have precise information on that score," said Pierre de Roncherolles. "Monsieur le Cardinal has summoned to Paris all those regiments whose commanders are, or so he believes, loyal to him: the Chartres Regiment, the Calais Regiment, the Anjou Regiment, the Queen's Light Horse –"

"All the better, all the better!" cried the Chevalier de Lansac. "That being so, we'll seize the provinces without bloodshed."

"Ashtaroth, the devil of greed," Turlupin continued in a whisper. "Tipheret, the devil of fornication; Sathael, through whom sin entered Paradise."

"I admire your erudition," said Monsieur de Bragelone. "Back home in Poitou we have another nobleman versed in such sciences. He has had a book printed in which he proves the triune nature of God on wholly scientific grounds."

"I know the names of the guardians of the celestial throne," Turlupin boasted, "likewise those of the most renowned Roman generals. I also know a remedy for palpitations of the heart, scabies, consumption, hernia, and paralysis. Furthermore, I know a way of making partridges so drunk that one can catch them by hand."

"I, too, am acquainted with that method," said Monsieur de Bragelone. "You take some wheaten flour steeped in good vintage wine, fashion it into pellets, and scatter them on the ground. I was told that by an old gamekeeper who died last winter."

"For my part," said Turlupin, "I had it from Maria, the sister of Mosis, a very learned Jewess."

"Learned she may be," said the country gentleman, "but she knows little about game. Those pellets are of scant use, believe me. Scatter them and you may catch a few tipsy sparrows, but never a partridge. Partridges are cunning, they won't be duped by such a trick. Myself, I prefer to shoot them."

"You came all the way from Flanders," the Prince d'Aubijoux called across the table, "and never met with a single adventure?"

"Others may carry a consecrated thaler with St Agatha's head on it," Monsieur de Caille et de Rougon said to his neighbour, the Vicomte d'Aubeterre, "but Le Dangereux has his pact with Satan. He denies it – he dislikes one to speak of it – but I've seen the document itself. He keeps it hidden in his sleeve."

"Adventure? I had but one," Le Dangereux replied. "Midway between Marles and Soissons I was recognized by the governor's guards and detained for three hours at an inn, the 'Renard Rusé'. The landlord had cause to regret it. I set the roof ablaze and took advantage of the subsequent confusion to make off. The rest is not worth mentioning. Latterly, not half an hour since, six ruffians set on me down by the river bank, a musket-shot distant from this house."

"Only six?" Monsieur de la Roche-Pichemer interposed. "Had they been sixteen, Le Dangereux, you'd still have scorned them."

"Six came, five escaped. One of them I put paid to. Monsieur le Cardinal should employ better workmen."

"Gentlemen," said the Duc de Lavan, "the rain has eased. This game bird Le Dangereux dispatched on the river bank – shall we inspect it?"

"You'll find him where the path turns inland from the embankment," Le Dangereux told him. "I had my back against the trunk of a poplar, so he must be lying beneath it."

"I'm with you," said Monsieur de la Roche-Pichemer.

"And I!" came a simultaneous cry from Prince de Marsillac and Monsieur de Berteauville.

"I too," said Monsieur de Bragelone. He turned to Turlupin. "And you, Monsieur? Will you join us?"

Turlupin hadn't heard a word of the conversation. "I'm weary," he said. "I've been on my feet since early this morning."

"Just a brief nocturnal stroll along the river bank," said Monsieur de Bragelone.

"Oh, in that case, I'll come too," Turlupin exclaimed happily. His fatigue disappeared in an instant, for that was the spot where he hoped to meet his friend the scrivener.

[18]

MONSIEUR DE LA Roche-Pichemer, sword in hand, went on ahead with the Duc de Lavan's equerry, who carried a blazing torch. Four noblemen and Turlupin followed at a distance, for fear of an ambuscade, and two lackeys armed with loaded muskets brought up the rear.

Not a star could be seen. The icy wind that swept across the wide expanse of grass was wafting pale skeins of mist from the river, and the leafless twigs of the bushes on the bank were thick with hoarfrost. When the path rounded a bend, the lighted windows of the house vanished in a trice, as if a puff of wind had extinguished the candles in every room.

While they were making their way along the embankment, Monsieur de Berteauville recounted the lamentable story of a nobleman who had ventured out of camp on a pitch-black night such as this. It had happened, he explained in a low voice, during the last Spanish campaign.

"Finding himself in the midst of a flock of sheep being driven across a bridge to Mirenoix, the worthy man mistook them in the darkness for an enemy outpost. More than a little dismayed, he went down on his knees, threw up his hands, and cried out, "Have mercy, good cavalrymen! Spare my life, I surrender!"

His words were drowned by the hiss and gurgle of the river, but no one was listening to him in any case. The Duc de Lavan had paused and was peering left and right.

"There are now only four of us," he said. "Monsieur de Josselin! What the devil has become of Monsieur de Josselin?"

Turlupin, eager to seek the scrivener's advice but anxious lest his aristocratic friends should see him go, had taken advantage of the darkness to sneak off.

"He was beside me a moment ago," said Monsieur de Bragelone.

"Walk on, walk on!" cried Monsieur de Berteauville. "I'm freezing – my shoes are full of water. He'll rejoin us soon enough."

He fell to cursing because the ceaseless rainstorms of recent days had turned the footpath into a quagmire. Suddenly a voice rang out – a voice that belonged neither to Monsieur de la Roche-Pichemer nor to the equerry.

"Halt! Stay where you are! Not another step!"

"Forward! They're at grips!" cried the Duc de Lavan. "Quickly, help them!"

The four noblemen drew their swords and hurried in the direction indicated by the reddish torchlight, followed by the brace of lackeys.

The figures of two men loomed up out of the mist. Their pikes were levelled at Monsieur de la Roche-Pichemer's chest, but their faces were eloquent of the consternation they felt at being so suddenly and so thoroughly outnumbered. A third figure lay at their feet. From the river, where the dark shape of a boat could just be seen bobbing on the wavelets, came a gentle plashing sound.

Nonchalantly, without deigning even to glance at his potential adversaries, Monsieur de la Roche-Pichemer thrust their pikes aside. Then he said, "Equerry, shine a light on his face."

The torchlight illumined the leaden face of the man on the ground, which was twisted with pain. The pikemen continued to hold their weapons poised, ready to do battle against the odds, but no one heeded them.

"Croiseau! It's Croiseau, by heaven!" cried La Roche-Pichemer. "It's Croiseau, the one they call the 'Pack-horse' – the most villainous of all the blackguards in the Cardinal's service."

"It is indeed," said the Duc de Lavan. "There's retribution for you! It was he that sent the Master of the Horse and Monsieur de Thou to the scaffold."

"Well, Croiseau," said La Roche-Pichemer, chuckling grimly, "how do you come to be lying here? What butcher's hook did you run into in the dark?"

"Poor Croiseau," said Prince de Marsillac, "you're all bloody. Who bathed you so roughly?"

One of the pikemen lowered his weapon.

"Gentlemen," he said, "for poor folk like us, life is a cruel dilemma: die of hunger or become a rogue. Many was the day when the man you see lying here could not find even a mouthful of bread for his children. But you, whose wealth makes you great – who compelled you to turn traitor and rebel?"

"My friend," said Prince de Marsillac, "no one can answer you that. For all the discoveries that have been made, many a province of the human soul remains uncharted territory."

"Ah, it's Monsieur le Prince de Marsillac!" exclaimed the other pikeman. "I didn't recognize Your Excellency till now. So you've left the castle at Angoulême, which the King assigned you as a residence."

"Run to the Cardinal and bring him word," said the Duc de Lavan. "It'll earn you ten pistoles for a surety."

A faint groan came from the grass at their feet. The wounded man opened his eyes.

"Is there a priest among you?" he asked.

"We brought none with us," Monsieur de la Roche-Pichemer replied. "You should have prayed to St Barbara not to let you die unshriven. Now it's too late – you're done for. Entreat St Peter to admit you to heaven."

The wounded man raised his head and glared at La Roche-Pichemer with hatred.

"Then may you all pray to St Barbara," he cried, the breath rattling in his throat. "Your time is up. The day that's breaking – do you know its name? It's called St Martin's Day. Before twice times twelve hours have passed, France will have taken on another aspect – a better one."

He groaned and pressed his hands to his chest.

"What does he mean?" Monsieur de Berteauville asked uneasily.

The Duc de Lavan threw back his head and laughed in the carefree way he had.

"The charlatans and street musicians, the pamphleteers and rhymesters and all the mean and worthless folk of Paris have made an assignation for today. They call their meeting the shuttlecock tournament – why, no one knows. They themselves are ignorant of the reason. No respectable citizen has any part in the affair."

At that moment Turlupin emerged from the gloom. He elbowed one of the lackeys aside to see what was afoot. As soon as he caught sight of the wounded man and perceived the innumerable wrinkles in the leaden face, he recognized the moribund form as that of the scrivener whom he had vainly been seeking on the river bank – the ally on whose aid and counsel all his hopes had been founded.

He bent, motionless, over the dying man,

"Have a care, Monsieur de Josselin!" the Duc de Lavan said warningly. "Don't venture too near. Croiseau is treacherous. He could drive his dagger into your throat with his last breath."

The dying man strove to sit up, only to sink back with a groan.

"Monsieur de Josselin is dead," he cried with the last ounce of strength afforded him by the life that was ebbing away. "Monsieur de Josselin lies at the bottom of the river."

A momentary silence fell. Nothing could be heard but the whisper of the reeds and the lapping of water against the boat. Then the duke's clear young voice rang out.

"He's delirious. Monsieur de Josselin is alive and standing here beside me, heaven be praised."

Not another word escaped the dying man's lips. His two friends picked him up and carried him down to their boat. The noblemen retraced their steps in silence.

Up in the gallery of the great house, where footmen bearing candles were waiting to escort each guest to his room, Monsieur de la Roche-Pichemer turned to the Duc de Lavan.

"Odd of Croiseau to have said that Monsieur de Josselin is dead," he remarked. "I wonder what gave him such a notion."

And he looked thoughtfully, searchingly, into Turlupin's face, which was pale as death.

[19]

THE DAY WAS far advanced when Turlupin awoke. His eye instinctively sought the Widow Sabot's tapestry, with its faded portrayal of Queen Judith, but all he could discern were outlandish beasts, armed men, and a naked woman: the sorceress Circe seated at her loom in a spacious hall with mountain wolves and lions pressing affectionately about her. Eurylochus, Odysseus' friend, was striding across the threshold with his brazen-armoured companions, and the whole scene was bathed in the blood-orange rays of a painted sun.

What puzzled him most of all, however, was the wig he saw lying on an ebony table inlaid with tortoise-shell, malachite and lapis lazuli. Last night he had thrown himself down on the bed fully dressed, but the wig, which he found unfamiliar and bothersome, he had deposited on the table in the dark. And now, in his somnolent state, he couldn't fathom how it had found its way from the barbershop to his bedchamber. Such was the inexplicable and anomalous phenomenon to which his first waking thoughts were addressed.

Then he noticed the sword at his side and the plumed hat that had fallen to the floor, and the events of the previous night came back to him. At the same time, there awoke in him the memory of a dream that had oppressed and alarmed him in his sleep.

He saw himself, the first-born son of the ducal house of Lavan, promenading through the streets of Paris in all his finery, complete with plumed hat and sword, while his wretched younger brother stood far off with mule and handbell, piteously crying, "Plumed hats! Who'll buy my plumed hats?" And he, Turlupin, strode proudly on. The common folk stood reverently aside for him, galloping horsemen saluted him, beauteous ladies waved to him from gleaming, gilded carriages. But all at once he heard a voice – the voice of little Nicole.

"Turlupin!" he heard her call. "That's our Turlupin, with a plumed hat and a sword! Look sharp, Monsieur Turlupin – run, you're late."

Gone were the horsemen, gone the gleaming, gilded carriages and the deferential crowd and the plumed hat and sword; Turlupin was back in the barbershop with a razor in his hand, and Monsieur Pigeot the dyer was frowning at him.

"You know how to while away the time, eh? You go for a stroll, you greet your friends, you gossip – yes, and what about my wig, eh?"

Turlupin got up and went to the window, and memories of the nocturnal vision faded as he looked out at the light of day. Little Nicole, the barbershop, the razor, Monsieur Pigeot's wig – he had left them all far behind. He was Turlupin no longer. No one knew his secret. The scrivener who had transformed him into Monsieur de Josselin could never give him away: his lips were sealed for ever.

All that still preyed on his mind was fear of the duel he would have to fight with Monsieur de la Roche-Pichemer. For a while he stood at the window filled with dismal forebodings. Then that anxiety, too, subsided.

"Madame, my noble mother!" he said, smiling happily. "Why didn't I think of her right away? I still haven't spoken with her. I'll go to her at once and tell her everything, and she'll help me. She won't permit that scoundrel to skewer me on his sword."

A sudden sound made him look round. Standing in the doorway, dressed all in white, was the chambermaid appointed to wait on him.

"What do you wish to order for breakfast, Excellency?"

Turlupin was hungry. He would have liked to ask for a slice of bread and some soft cheese, that being his usual holiday fare, but he knew what was proper to his rank.

"Pray bring me some milk soup with biscuits," he replied, "and to follow a slice of game pie, well truffled and not too small."

The chambermaid withdrew. Turlupin sank down on a chair, thoroughly displeased with himself. He had blundered, he realized, and it was too late to make amends. He had mentioned only food, not wine, and a nobleman would surely empty a bottle or two of burgundy with his breakfast.

But the chambermaid returned bearing a tray laden not only with a bowl of steaming milk soup, some biscuits, and a whole game pie, but with two bottles of wine as well. She laid the table and stationed herself beside Turlupin in readiness to wait on him while he ate.

Turlupin began spooning up the milk soup.

"Where is Madame?" he inquired. "I wish to speak with her."

"Madame has yet to return from Mass," the girl replied, "but we expect her at any minute. Do you prefer burgundy or claret?"

"Let me know when she returns," said Turlupin. "I have something of the utmost importance to tell her. Pour me a drop of the white and as much as you please of the red."

She filled one glass with claret and another with burgundy and set a slice of game pie before him. Turlupin studied her face. He found her more beautiful than any girl he had ever met. Her eyes, he suddenly saw, were brimming with tears. He ate a mouthful of pie and took a sip of wine. Then he said, "You seem distressed for some reason."

The girl hung her head.

"Ah, Excellency," she said, "I didn't come to burden you with my troubles."

"Nonsense, speak out," Turlupin told her. "I'll listen while I eat and drink."

"You're very kind, Excellency," the girl said. "Well, since you permit me to tell you the truth: I intend to leave this house tomorrow morning, and I fear I may be compelled to earn my living by spinning wool."

"But why?" Turlupin demanded, cramming himself with as much game pie as he could manage. "Why leave a house so plentifully provided with everything imaginable?"

"The steward has taken it into his head to marry me to one of the lackeys, and I've more reason than one to abominate the man he has allotted me as a husband. I cannot rightly describe his appearance. He has a flat face and thick legs and eyes like a pig, and he's old and cantankerous and miserly into the bargain. He lacks all the makings of a true lover, but the steward says he'll make me a good husband."

Turlupin was indignant. "And this loathsome creature has the effrontery to love you?" he exclaimed. "Is there no way of deterring him?"

"None," the girl replied sadly. "He pesters me unceasingly. As for the steward, I cannot live at peace with him since he embarked on this scheme."

Turlupin, oblivious of the wine and the pie, was thinking hard. If anyone could help this poor girl, it was he. He had only to put in a word for her with his mother, Madame la Duchesse.

"I don't know what has inspired me with such a feeling of friendship for you," he said. "Suffice it to say, I'm determined to do my best for you. That impudent rogue of a steward! I shall inform Madame la Duchesse of his outrageous conduct. We'll show him who we are. Madame will listen to me, rest assured of that. Ah, I could tell you things that would amaze you!"

"If you would indeed speak to Madame on my behalf,

Excellency," the girl said delightedly, "you would make me happier than I deserve or dare to hope. I should be most grateful to you, Excellency. Having tried hitherto to give you every reason for satisfaction, I shall in future devote myself to your service with even greater care."

"Very well," said Turlupin. "First let me speak with Madame la Duchesse. May I be flogged if anything in this house fails to accord with my wishes from now on! Tell me your name. I must know what you're called if I'm to plead your cause with Madame."

"My name is Jeanneton," the chambermaid said, "but there's another of that name in the house, so they call me Guérarde. I come from Boulogne. My father has a small joiner's workshop in that town, but he's quite elderly and customers call on him very seldom. I went to Paris so as not to be a burden to him, and I've eaten the bread of this house since my sixteenth year."

"From Boulogne? That surprises me," said Turlupin. "Most girls from the neighbourhood of Boulogne have hair that's dry and altogether lacking in lustre. That's on account of the sea air, which bleaches hair and makes it brittle, but yours is a handsome shade of chestnut and curls of its own accord. It's unusual to find a girl from Boulogne with hair of such beauty."

"It's true," the girl agreed with great alacrity, "my hair is curly by nature, but you, Excellency, are the first guest to have noticed it. The others pay it no heed at all."

"You're young and shapely," Turlupin went on. "I admire those qualities. Pray take a drop of wine and sample this game pie."

"With your permission, sir, and only so as not to offend you," said the girl. She picked up a glass and sipped it.

Neither of them spoke for a while. A drop of wine trembled on her lower lip. Turlupin edged closer, wondering how best to proclaim his love for this beautiful girl in a manner that was not only seemly but appropriate to a nobleman.

"I would give anything to storm that barricade of yours," he said at last, rather diffidently, pointing to her bodice.

She blushed and glanced at the open door, then bent over him.

"Excellency," she whispered shyly, "it's said that the love of a fine gentleman like you bestows no happiness or prosperity on a poor girl like me, but you've been so kind. If you truly fancy me, I sleep in the embroideresses' chamber, and I'm also to be found there in the afternoons. It's the third door along the narrow passage that leads from the gallery to this part of the house. If you retire to your room after the midday meal, knock on that door as you pass and I'll come to you."

"Guérarde," said Turlupin, filled with delighted anticipation, "I'm exceedingly fond of you. You've made me the happiest man alive, and I thank God that he created you as beautiful as you are."

"Don't call me Guérarde, call me Jeanneton. Another thing, Excellency: you must knock twice so that I'll know it's you, for Captain de Caille et de Rougon is here again. That old man keeps pestering me to become the object of his caresses, which are more like those of an ape than a human being. So for safety's sake, Excellency, knock twice on the door. Then I'll know it's –"

She broke off because the steward had appeared in the doorway. Picking up the trayful of bottles, plates and glasses, she hurried from the room.

"Your Excellency," the steward announced, "the meeting has just begun – you're awaited in the Moorish Chamber. Have all your needs been satisfactorily attended to?"

[20]

RESPECTFUL SILENCE REIGNED in the Moorish Chamber as Pierre de Roncherolles, last surviving witness of a great and vanished age, rose to his feet. Thirty years before, at the last meeting of the Estates General, this old aristocrat had answered the king in the name of the French nobility with a proud defiance that had never been forgotten. Now he ceremoniously welcomed all present, addressing each man by name and thanking him for his attendance.

"I was sent here by the Norman nobility," he went on, "the nobility of a land whose walls are the waves of the deep and whose roof is the tempest. They dared to set a governor over us, one who was not our equal, not of the nobility. For as long as he was merely unjust – for as long as he curtailed public liberties and stripped us of our posts and offices, fiefs and estates – we bore our misfortunes uncomplainingly and persevered in our resolve to await better times. Now, however, it has become unmistakably clear to all that our honour is in jeopardy."

The big room rang with cries of outrage and indignation. Turlupin turned to his neighbour, Prince de Marsillac.

"I don't see Monsieur de la Roche-Pichemer. Where is he?"

"Gone to the Louvre to see if there's any news."

"Will he return before nightfall?"

"Without a doubt," the prince replied.

Meantime, the hubbub had subsided sufficiently for Pierre de Roncherolles to continue his speech.

"We in Normandy desire peace. So does the king, so does the queen, so do the common folk and all France, but Cardinal Richelieu does not desire peace. For years on end he has continually overruled the laws of the realm by force, heedless of the vested and attested rights of the nobility. He desires war. Very well, he shall have it! We shall take up arms against the tyrant who has broken the laws, ravaged France, and sent His Majesty's noblest and truest vassals to the scaffold. And, just as the Virgin and St Joseph –"

"Long live the memory of Monsieur d'Effiat! Long live the memory of Monsieur de Montmorency!" cried Prince d'Aubijoux.

"And," Monsieur de Roncherolles pursued, raising his voice, "just as the Virgin and St Joseph went forth to seek the Christ Child, so shall we go forth and emblazon our banners with the words *Regem nostrum quærimus*! – we seek our king, our rightful king, the king that heeds us, the king devoid of despotism and tyranny, the king without Richelieu. I am done. May God bless our undertaking and preside over our deliberations, so that all our decisions contribute to his glory and the furtherance of his kingdom."

The ensuing hush, a tribute to the venerable leader of the Norman nobility, did not last long. It was replaced by a faint commotion and excited whispers as the floor was claimed by the envoy from Auvergne, Monsieur de Chaudenier, Marquis de Rochechouart and Knight of the Order of the Holy Ghost. The Duc de Lavan rose and made his way silently across the room. Beside the noblemen clustered around Prince d'Aubijoux he paused as if he had some confidential information to impart.

"You know me well enough," Monsieur de Chaudenier began, "to know that my actions have never, throughout my life, been prompted by fear, and that, whatever I have done, honour has been my sole concern. I have always advised that we should exhaust all means of reconciliation and take up arms only in the very last resort. As I see it, that day has yet to come."

"That day has indeed come!" cried Prince d'Aubijoux. "The time for waiting is past!"

"That day has yet to come," Monsieur de Chaudenier repeated, but his words evoked noisy denials on all hands.

"Don't heed him! Further delay will spell defeat and ruination."

"The Cardinal laughs at our tardiness and turns it to his own advantage."

"Are we to give him time to hatch new plots?"

Monsieur de Chaudenier began again. "The nobles of Auvergne, whose delegate I am –"

"Enough! We'll hear no more of it!"

"Delay and more delay, that's a faintheart's policy!"

"The nobles of Auvergne, whose delegate I am," Monsieur de Chaudenier shouted above the din, "are entitled to your attention. Love of war and danger is their ruling passion, honour their religion. I demand a hearing!"

"Silence for the delegate from Auvergne!" boomed Monsieur Le Coqu-Corbeille.

The Duc de Lavan materialized beside Turlupin. He laid a hand on his shoulder and whispered in his ear.

"Monsieur de Josselin, yesterday you did me the honour of assuring me of your goodwill. The alliance is now in question. I hope to see you, being a friend, on our side."

"Prince d'Aubijoux proclaims that the day has come," the delegate from Auvergne continued. "Well then, gentlemen, a question: Are we prepared for that day? We can muster noblemen and armed peasants in plenty, I grant you, but where are the munitions – where are the magazines required to furnish those troops with all they need? Do we have the provincial governors on our side? Do we possess even one fortress capable of holding out for longer than two days? Sedan, Libourne, Turasson, Limeuil – all these are lost to us."

"Monsieur de Chaudenier forgets something," cried the Duc de Lavan. "He forgets that we have friends who are only waiting for a word from us to hasten to our assistance with all the forces they can raise."

Utter silence followed those words, and in the midst of that silence, pale with dismay, Monsieur de Caille et de Rougon rose to his feet.

"Everyone knows how greatly I venerate the person of the King of Spain," he said, his voice trembling with agitation, "and no one knows better than I how greatly such assistance would benefit our undertaking. But, God help me, I tell you this plainly: Let each of you act as his conscience commands; for my own part, I cannot in honour fight shoulder to shoulder with the enemies of my native land."

The assembled noblemen, who were all at one in their hatred of Richelieu, promptly divided into two factions: on the left, some clustered around Prince d'Aubijoux; on the right, others took their lead from Monsieur de Caille et de Rougon. Between them, utterly bewildered and perplexed, stood Turlupin. He vainly scanned the turbulent scene for the Duc de Lavan, not knowing which side his host would wish him to join.

Meanwhile, furious cries flew back and forth between the two camps:

"If we win, we shall have done well by our native land. Any means to that end is justified!"

"A plague on the house of Austria! A plague on that scoundrel, Chancellor Olivares!"

"A just peace between the crowns of Spain and France for the good of Christendom, that's our desire!"

"I refuse to countenance any pact or treaty with our country's enemies!"

"They deny us justice. We must obtain it for ourselves by each and every means!"

"Monsieur de Noirmoutier, once upon a time, before you lost all sense of moderation – "

"Herr von Mömpelgard, to show you that I fear you as little as I respect you –"

"You call it politics; I call it treason!"

"Who dares to call me a traitor?"

The uproar ceased abruptly. All eyes had turned to the Duc de Noirmoutier and Graf von Mömpelgard, who were confronting each other sword in hand. Turlupin, fancying himself in mortal danger from the pair of them, hastily retired to the door.

"You dared to call me a traitor," yelled the Duc de Noirmoutier, beside himself with rage. "God's blood, if I didn't know –"

"A traitor, yes, and forsworn to boot!" Graf von Mömpelgard yelled back. "What's more, I'm ready to recommend a hermitage where you can conceal your ignominy from the eyes of the world."

Just as the two adversaries seemed about to launch themselves at each other, Turlupin saw the door open an inch or two. Little Jeanneton's inquiring face appeared in the crack. Catching sight of him, she signified that she had something to impart. Turlupin slunk out unheeded and quietly closed the door behind him.

"They've gone mad in there," he told the girl. "They'll be coming to blows at any minute – indeed, two of them are about to kill each other. A pity about that German nobleman. I heard him curse and sing last night, and he's better at both than all the rest."

"Excellency," Jeanneton whispered, "it was very imprudent of me to come here – we're strictly forbidden to enter this part of the house while the meeting lasts – but you asked me to let you know when Madame returned from Mass. If you're quick, Excellency, you'll meet her on the stairs."

* * *

Slowly, staring into space, the Duchesse de Lavan ascended the stairs followed by two of her ladies-in-waiting, who watched her every movement with keen attention. Autumnal sunbeams pierced the tall, round-arched windows and fell on the white marble balustrade.

Turlupin stood motionless on the top step. He saw his mother in her widow's weeds, saw her face and the eyes that had dwelled on him in church. Impassioned words of affection hovered on his lips – words that had awaited this solemn moment for many a long year – but he restrained himself and said nothing. It was for his mother to speak first.

He doffed his hat, and the lock of white hair fell across his brow.

The Duchesse de Lavan walked straight past him without turning her head, as if he did not exist.

[21]

A YOUNG SCULLION RAN down the stairs with a spit in his hand, paused, looked back, and hurried on. A door closed, silence returned. The shadows of two birds frolicking outside in the autumn sunlight flitted across the marble steps.

Turlupin awoke as if from trance and gradually recovered his wits. How long had he been standing there with his plumed hat doffed in salutation? How long was it since his mother had walked past him like a stranger?

He felt neither sorrowful nor surprised, just infinitely forlorn. He shook his head and sighed.

"I vexed her," he told himself with a melancholy smile. "She was startled to see me – she thought I'd come to betray her secret. She was afraid that everyone would learn that she, a high-born duchess, has a son who measures folk for wigs. That's why she affected not to see me."

He stared at the floor. His face darkened, his heart brimmed with proud defiance.

"She has my picture and that's enough for her – she has no desire to see me in the flesh! Very well, she needn't worry: I'll go and never cross her path again. What a fool I was to believe that a wig-maker can transform himself into a duke overnight! Anyway, is it such a boon to be a great lord? Posing as a nobleman in this house has brought me nothing but fear, danger, and a host of embarrassments. My mother doesn't care to set eyes on me – I'm too humble for her liking. What is there to keep me here?

Nothing! Monsieur de la Roche-Pichemer can find another person to fight with. I'm sick of it all – I'm off!"

Then he remembered the chambermaid, who had also resolved to leave the house like himself, and his anger yielded to thoughts of a more agreeable nature.

"We'll go together. Little Jeanneton with her brown plaits! I didn't come here in vain after all – I've found someone who loves me. We were brought together by God himself. It's better I'm not a nobleman, for if two people are to live happily together they must be of the same rank. She'll be astounded when I tell her I'm not Monsieur de Josselin, just a wig-maker, albeit one that knows his trade and has learned how to make other folk's sous his own in an honest manner. She'll have no need to spin wool. I'll bestir myself – I'll make enough to keep us both."

And he began to picture the course his life would take in Boulogne, for he had no wish to return to the Widow Sabot's.

"Her father has a joiner's workshop, but it earns him little. Very well, I'll turn his joiner's workshop into a barbershop. Folk will come flocking in as soon as they see that I've a thorough knowledge of my craft, and that I can trim their beards in the Greek, Spanish or Italian manner. Besides, it's always good for business when an establishment boasts a pretty young woman who knows how to pass the time of day with customers. Jeanneton can sit there and take the money. Later on I'll show her how to mix hair to get the right colour, and the old man can help if his fingers are deft enough. I must buy a hair drum, and some combs and scissors, and a copper boiler for heating water, and some crimping tongs, and a vice, and some boxwood curlers, and a plaiting board, and smoothing irons, and a barber's whetstone, and razors. All those things will cost money . . ."

Pensively, he examined the plumed hat in his hand.

"This hatband set with blue stones – it's bound to be worth

a hundred livres or more. And the dagger and sword and lace trimmings and silken ribbons – I've no need of any of those, so I'll turn them into money. That should be enough. But where's that coat of mine? Damnation, I left it draped over my chair upstairs – pray God it hasn't disappeared! I must go back there and see . . ."

He hurried back into the great chamber.

The kingdom's most eminent men, who were debating the future destiny of France, were joined there by a journeyman barber eager to find his coat with a view to pawning it.

The plan for an alliance with Spain had foundered on the fierce opposition of a small minority. Monsieur de Caille et de Rougon was being congratulated by his friends. Graf von Mömpelgard and the Duc de Noirmoutier were standing peaceably side by side, having arranged to fight a duel in the pinewood at Vincennes that afternoon.

The debate proceeded. Consideration was to be given to other ways of overthrowing the cardinal's tyrannical regime. Monsieur d'Hunauldaye rose from among his friends.

"The cardinal is hatching new conspiracies," he began. "Rumours are rife throughout the city. Everyone has heard them, but no one knows his true intentions. He smiles whenever he encounters one of our number. Has he obtained the King's permission to replenish the jails? Has he secured the consent of Parliament and the courts to our sentences of death? It's enough that he goes around as if victory were already his. We must steal a march on him. My friends and I are agreed that it's time to stake everything on a single throw. One way or another, we must rid ourselves of the man."

"Your pardon, sir," Turlupin whispered to the Vicomte d'Aubeterre, who was occupying the chair over which he had draped his coat.

Monsieur d'Hunauldaye proceeded to set forth his plan in a stream of excited words.

"My friends and I meet at the 'Trois Alouettes' tavern. From there, unseen ourselves, we observe the Cardinal's mansion. It's nine o'clock in the morning. Everyone knows his allotted task. Two of our number keep watch at the street corners to guard against surprises. The cardinal drives out. At a given signal we surround the carriage. 'Halt! Don't move!' Two of us seize the horses' reins, two more wrench open the carriage doors, I myself deliver the lethal blow, Lansac and Saint-Aignan cover my rear –"

His words were drowned by uproarious laughter. The Duc de Nevers rose and called for silence.

"And the Scottish Guards, Monsieur Hothead?" he said, stroking his grizzled beard. "What of the cardinal's Scottish Guards? Would they stand by and look on? Besides, he'll have Marshal de la Force with him in the carriage –"

"That's not the way!" cried Monsieur de la Magdelaine. "No, not in the streets of Paris! He must be ambushed in open countryside."

Turlupin, who had been listening to every word, was paralysed with terror.

"It's downright murder, this plan of theirs," he muttered. "What temerity! Is it permitted to say such things? And here I am, listening to them! The fools, the madcaps, they'll talk themselves to the gallows with such speeches, and me into the bargain, and there'll be no one to have a Mass said for me. Murder, ambush – no, I'll have none of it. I'm off."

The floor had now been claimed by Monsieur de Berteauville, the delegate of the Burgundian nobility.

"I'm told the cardinal inspects his Scottish Guards every week," he said. "If one of his officers could be prevailed on to loose off a shot by accident –"

"I've heard nothing, God preserve me," Turlupin muttered in horror, "– nothing."

Having retrieved his coat, he hurriedly threaded his way toward the door. Then he broke into a run as if the bailiffs were already at his heels. He did not regain his composure until he reached the narrow passage that led from the gallery to the wing in which his room was situated.

"This is where I'll find her," he told himself. "She must leave with me at once. No one should make such speeches. I'll not stay a moment longer – I've no wish to end in the galleys. The third door, then knock twice so she knows it's me. She'll be astonished when I tell her who I am and say I'm going with her to Boulogne and we'll stay together. There's only one thing: she'll think she has to regale me every day with a breakfast of biscuits and pies, but no, I'm not the kind of man who prizes a good meal above all else. I'm content enough if I find a piece of mutton in my midday dish of turnips, and a pitcher of wine a day will suffice the two of us . . ."

He pricked up his ears at a sudden sound: a woman was walking slowly towards him along the dim, narrow passage.

He recognized her as the Duchesse de Lavan, and all at once it struck him: his mother was alone – no one stood between him and her – so he could bid her farewell. He was going, he was leaving the house in which his cradle had stood. Once, just once, he wanted to speak to his mother.

The Duchesse de Lavan paused and listened as he hurried towards her.

"It's me," he faltered, unable to repress the words that escaped his lips. "It's me, Madame, your son. Give me your blessing."

She raised her hand and ran it lightly over his face, first the right cheek, then the left, then his forehead.

A door opened and footsteps approached. Tearing himself away, Turlupin turned and sped off.

Tumultuous, turbulent emotions seethed within him. His mother had blessed him – his mother had stroked his face. Gone were all thoughts of poor Jeanneton and the humble but happy life he had meant to make for them both. Fate had summoned him to this house. Here he belonged, and here he must remain.

His mother had blessed him. Even were this day to be his last, his fear of death had vanished. He squared his shoulders. Utterly transformed, he retraced his steps with the sword clanking at his side.

A poor little wig-maker had fearfully, timidly slunk from the great chamber. The man who re-entered it was the first-born son of the Duc de Lavan, ready and willing to take his rightful place among the nobility of France.

[22]

All eyes were fixed on Le Dangereux. The great strategist was boldly delineating the campaign that would end the cardinal's sanguinary regime and restore the power and glory of the nobility.

"We shall engage mercenaries in Lorraine and Flanders. For that purpose we already have at our disposal a hundred and sixty thousand livres, partly in silver coin, partly in double pistoles. That will suffice to recruit four thousand men. A further three hundred thousand livres must be raised for the maintenance of that force. Waging war costs money. If you wish to see me dance, you must pay the fiddler."

He slapped the hilt of his sword and laughed. Speaking on behalf of the viscounty of Turenne, the Vicomte d'Entragues declared his willingness to guarantee the said sum.

"We cross the frontier," Le Dangereux continued, "and thenceforth we're the royal army. We make for the capital by forced marches. Meantime, the nobility of the Île de France will assemble at Corbeil and seize the bridge at Villeneuve-St-Georges, that being the place I intend to make the midpoint of my dispositions."

"We're resolved to obey you to the letter," the delegate from the Île de France assured him.

"There I shall await the enemy. The terrain, with its gulleys, hills and watercourses, will afford me every advantage and enable me to rout the vanguard of the opposing force before it has time to deploy. Possession of the bridge will further enable me to attack the enemy in the rear and catch him between two fires. Being an experienced soldier, Marshal de la Meilleray, who commands the cardinal's troops, will disengage and withdraw as soon as he perceives his predicament. I shall pursue him. Paris will open its gates to him, whereupon I shall cut off the city's supplies of food by land and water."

"Meanwhile," interjected the Duc de Nevers, "Marshal de Guiche will advance from Orleans to raise the siege."

"True," said Le Dangereux, "and Monsieur d'Hocquincourt's troops will bear down on us from Troyes. We shall be done for unless we contrive to seize the city and the cardinal's person before the relieving armies appear outside the walls of Paris. We have no heavy artillery and the city is heavily fortified, but two hundred and fifty thousand people dwell within its walls. Two days without bread, and they'll compel the cardinal to open the gates to us. A daily ration of one-and-a-half pounds of bread is required to keep a person alive. It follows that –"

"Oho!" the Chevalier de Lansac exclaimed. "I give my servants four pounds a day, not counting bread for soup."

"The blind folk in our almshouse get five gallons of wheat a year and still complain of hunger," said the Vicomte d'Aubeterre.

"Two pounds of bread, the same of meat, and a pint of wine," said Captain de Caille et de Rougon, "– that's a cavalryman's daily ration."

"I put it at one-and-a-half pounds of bread per head," Le Dangereux went on. "Assuming that one gallon of wheat yields two hundred pounds of bread, two thousand gallons a day are required to feed the entire city. The riverside granaries that supply Paris with wheat contain a hundred and twelve thousand gallons. Whatever else there may exist within the walls in the way of grain and flour, whether in bakeries, store-rooms or mills, will last for two days at the most. It is of paramount importance, therefore, that the two large mills and the granaries in the harbour be destroyed by fire as soon as our troops appear before the walls of the city. Which of you is prepared to risk his life in this venture, whose outcome will determine the success or failure of our entire campaign?"

"I am!" cried Turlupin.

The room fell silent. All eyes scanned the face of the man who had volunteered to undertake so perilous a mission.

The Duc de Lavan went over to Turlupin.

"Sir," he said respectfully, "I know of your fervent devotion to our cause and I thank you for this further proof of your fearlessness, but you're a stranger to this city. You're ignorant of the harbour and its hiding places, and it's vital to the success of our enterprise that –"

Turlupin cut him short. Electrified by the magnitude of his decision, he preferred to disclose his secret rather than be deprived of the glory that would accrue from such a feat.

"I know the city and its byways," he said. "I know the harbour and its hiding places as well as you yourself – as well as any man alive. I deceived you. It is not yet time for me to reveal my true name and lineage, but this much I can tell you: I'm not the man I have purported to be."

"I know that," called a voice from the doorway.

Monsieur de la Roche-Pichemer was leaning against the doorpost, one hand gripping his sword, the other pressing a cloth to his forehead. He swayed, and for a moment it seemed that he would fall. Monsieur de Berteauville, who was nearest the door, sprang to his assistance.

"He's bleeding," cried the Duc de Lavan. "Where have you been, Monsieur de la Roche-Pichemer? What news do you bring us?"

"Ill news for you and for us all," the nobleman replied. He lowered the cloth to reveal a wound running from temple to temple. "I hurried back to warn you, but it's too late. Let us take leave of one another. None of us will be alive an hour from now."

A babble of voices filled the air. Swords rattled, chairs crashed to the floor, Monsieur Le Coqu-Corbeille called for the equerry and his horse.

"Quiet!" called Monsieur Pierre de Roncherolles. "Be calm! Speak, Monsieur de la Roche-Pichemer. What has happened?"

La Roche-Pichemer drew himself erect and stood there, straight as a ramrod. Then he raised his sword and pointed in the direction of the city.

"Don't you hear?" he cried. "They're coming. The cardinal has allied himself with the common folk of Paris. They're on their way here now – they want our heads."

Another silence fell. The Duc de Lavan went to a window and threw it open. An icy gust of wind traversed the great chamber, and with it came a distant uproar: the tempestuous din of revolution.

[23]

TWENTY-SEVEN NOBLEMEN confronted the raging mob with drawn swords on the steps of the Hôtel Lavan. Their last hour had come and they knew it. All hope of escape was gone. Their one remaining thought was to preserve the honour of the nobility, their sole desire to fight off the rabble for as long as one of them still had breath in his body.

Death and destruction encompassed the house on every side. Between it and the river, the monstrous army of insurgents stood shoulder to shoulder in obedience to one man's will. A forest of pikes, oars, sickles and halberds bristled against the sky. Reinforcements poured in from all quarters, swelling the mob and redoubling its hatred.

On the right of the forecourt, hemmed in against the wall of the monastery garden, was a small detachment of the cardinal's Scottish Guards. Their commander had dismounted. His orders were to give the mob free rein as long as it refrained from turning its attention to the Augustinian monastery. He stood there in his carmine cloak, arms crossed and head resting against his charger's neck, as if, through his eyes, the Duc de Richelieu himself were witnessing the retribution that was about to overtake his opponents.

Up on the steps, the noblemen awaited the first onset.

"So many enemies," Graf von Mömpelgard remarked to Pierre de Roncherolles, "and nary a one with whom one could duel with sword or pistol."

The old doyen of the Norman nobility surveyed the mob with disdain.

"What an age!" he said. "Mice braving cold steel . . . We shall show them how a noblemen dies. May they see it and never forget!"

"Why do they hesitate?" cried the Duc de Lavan. "Why don't they attack?"

"My friend," Prince de Marsillac admonished him, "opening hostilities is an art in itself."

The Chevalier de Frontenac detached the white Maltese cross from his breast and kissed it.

"It is God's will," he said solemnly. "Let us cast ourselves into His arms and cry His holy name aloud. He alone can help us to attain Paradise."

Turlupin stood beside the stone parapet, sword in hand. His heart brimmed with pride and exultation at this opportunity to die a nobleman among noblemen after a life that had demeaned him in its ignominy, poverty and humiliation. His ancestral home, the house in which he had been born, was menaced by the fury of the canaille, and he was resolved to defend it.

Then he felt a hand on his shoulder. Monsieur de la Roche-Pichemer was standing beside him.

"Sir," said the wounded nobleman, his eyes burning with fever, "this morning the body of a man was found on the river bank. The ring on his finger bore the arms of Monsieur de Josselin. You gained entry to this house in the guise of a dead man. Now I see you on our side. Who are you, sir? Tell me your name."

Turlupin was in a quandary. He could not divulge the secret of his birth – he had to keep it to himself for his mother's sake – but Monsieur de la Roche-Pichemer suspected him to be a commoner.

"You're right, sir," he said at length. "I'm not the man you took me for. I cannot, even now, inform you of my true name and origins. I can tell you only this much, that the noblest of French blood flows in my –"

He broke off, and a look of horrified surprise dawned on his face. He had seen someone in the crowd who knew him as Turlupin – who knew him from the Widow Sabot's barbershop: Monsieur Gaspard was standing barely twenty paces away.

Not only was it Monsieur Gaspard beyond a doubt, but he had recognized him and was already opening his mouth to call out. "That's Turlupin," he would cry, "the wig-maker from the Rue des Apôtres! How does that wielder of curling tongs come to be among these noblemen?"

It couldn't be allowed to happen. This witness from the past must be silenced. Frantic with fear that Monsieur Gaspard would give him away, Turlupin performed the day's sole act of heroism.

Vaulting the parapet sword in hand, he hurled himself at the wall of humanity, burst through it, and fought his way past the two ranks of Seine bargemen who were protecting their leader. Nothing could stop him. Blows rained down on him, steel pierced his flesh, blood oozed from his temples, his shoulders, his breast. A sharp stab of pain shot through him. The next moment he was face to face with the Vicomte de Saint-Chéron, who had been on the point of giving the order to attack.

The two men recognized each other, yet they did not. The Vicomte de Saint-Chéron saw Turlupin, the barber who had trimmed his beard each week, and never guessed that what confronted him was the French nobility, a warrior caste bleeding to death from the thousand wounds inflicted on it by Richelieu and girding itself to strike a last, terrible blow against the modern age. As for Turlupin, he saw Monsieur Gaspard, the clothier's assistant from the Rue des Apôtres, who had bidden him a courteous good day on his weekly visits to the Widow Sabot's barbershop, and could not know that it was the French Revolution which sank to the ground in the person of the man whose breast he now transfixed with his blade, not to resurrect itself for another century-and-a-half.

The death of the Vicomte de Saint-Chéron ended the rebellion before it could begin.

Nothing happened at first, save that the dead man was surrounded by a shouting, jostling mob. Then terror seized the revolutionary horde. Leaderless now, it turned into a rabble of porters, janitors, carters, and discharged lackeys. Finding themselves embroiled in an armed confrontation with men who had for centuries been their lords and masters, they were suddenly aghast at their own audacity. Each began to fear for his life, and each sought to escape.

The retreat was transformed into a disorderly rout by an arquebusade from the upstairs windows, where Captain de Caille et de Rougon had stationed himself with the Duc de Lavan's armed grooms and coachmen. A quarter of an hour later the broad expanse of grass in front of the house was deserted. All that remained were caps, hats, cloaks, and discarded weapons.

Thus ended Monsieur de Saint-Chéron's grand shuttleclock tournament. It was Le Dangereux who had the final say that day. Pointing to the Scottish Guards, who were still stationed beside the monastery wall, he turned to Pierre de Roncherolles and said, "The festivities are at an end. Shouldn't we send the musicians home?" Then he went over to the detachment commander and doffed his hat.

"Sir," he said, bowing, "we're in for some rain, I fear. Your men will catch cold. Why not send them home?"

Turlupin had been deposited on the steps. His blood was staining the white marble, his life ebbing away. His one remaining wish was to see his mother.

"Madame!" he whispered.

The Duc de Lavan ran to fetch her, but Turlupin had breathed his last by the time she appeared.

"Madame," the young duke said to his mother, "this nobleman, who acquitted himself so bravely, desired to speak with you. He's dead. Did you know him, Madame?"

The Duchesse de Lavan, who had been blind since her sixteenth year, stooped and ran a hand over Turlupin's brow and cheeks. Then she shook her head.

"No," she said, her lifeless orbs staring into space. "No, I never knew him. But, may God forgive me, for a nobleman he had a very common face."

[24]

ON NOVEMBER 13TH, two days after Martinmas, Jacob Maugeret, a rogue and a thief by trade, returned to the village where he lived.

Maugeret had left Paris early that morning. He was tired and hungry, having trudged all of eleven miles and eaten nothing on the way save a handful of nuts.

Madame Maugeret, who was standing at the stove stirring a gruel of millet and panicum when he walked in, nodded to him.

"You're just in time," she said. "I didn't expect you home till Sunday. You'll be hungry, but there's enough here for us all, and I also have some bread in the house."

First, Maugeret stowed the tools of his trade in a chest: a length of cord with a hook on the end, two knives, a clubfoot jemmy, a little bag of poison pills for dogs, the lime-coated ravens' feathers he used to extract coins from offertory boxes, sundry picklocks, and the parish priest's testimonial he carried in token of his probity and poverty.

Then he went to the table and emptied out his thief's sack while Jacob, the elder of his two children, looked on.

"Not much of a haul this time," he said. "It isn't easy to go about one's business in Paris. The city's in a turmoil – everyone distrusts everyone else. What's more, folk have given up carrying their purses in their sleeves. Slit them open, and you find them empty."

His wife came over to the table with the spoon in her hand.

"A piece of canvas four ells long and two ells wide," said Maugeret. "A little jacket with ribbons on the sleeves – that's for Catherine. A bottle of oil. A pair of warm slippers made from cat's fur. A pewter plate. Two pigeons – those I killed with my stick. Five ells of silk ribbon in two colours. A tailor's measure – how that found its way into my sack I've no idea. Half a pound of soap – that wasn't easy to come by, the grocer was wary of me. Yes, my love, our trade demands more wit and skill than any other. A small silver pitcher. Money, too, but little enough – less than four livres in all."

The younger of the two children crept out of her corner, and Maugeret, who was waggish by nature, pulled his thief's sack over her head and said "Brrr!" as if he were the Devil.

"A big silver ladle," he went on. "A bone with some scraps of ham on it – that's for Sunday. A silver chain. A copper coal scuttle weighing seventeen pounds. I'm growing old – I need someone to accompany me and carry my sack, but young Jacob is no great walker as yet. Four silver buttons. Oh yes, and this trash here, which almost sent me to the gallows. I saw the chain around a fellow's neck and thought it was gold. Aha, I said to myself, that's as good as mine, but he noticed something and turned and seized me. Fortunately, it was in church during Mass, so he let me go sooner than make a noise. You can guess how quickly I made off! Yes, my love, that's how close I came to the gallows. I was frightened out of my wits, and for what? Look at it: mere copper, not a trace of gold. The whole thing wouldn't fetch so much as a sou."

And he scornfully tossed the medallion bearing the likenesses of Turlupin and Madame Sabot into the ashes on the hearth.

At the very same moment, the Widow Sabot was sitting in Monsieur Coquereau's grocer's shop. Little Nicole, who was also there, felt sad because she had been compelled to leave her cat behind at the barbershop. Monsieur Coquereau would tolerate no animals on his premises.

Madame Sabot was filling some little two-ounce bags with pepper, ginger, saffron and nutmeg, Monsieur Coquereau chewing dried plums as he counted the sous he had taken that day.

The widow sighed and rested her hands in her lap. The grocer looked up with a frown.

"You're still thinking of him," he said irritably. "The scoundrel doesn't deserve it, truly he doesn't. He took his coat and went off without even telling you where he was going."

"I'm very unhappy," the widow said, "but it consoles me that I enjoy your esteem, Monsieur Coquereau. If only I knew the reason for his going."

"Taverns exist and so do loose women," Monsieur Coquereau replied. "Need I say more?"

The widow shook her head.

"He was no drinker," she said. "Even a pint of wine a day was too much for him – he never drank more than that. Till yesterday I would have sworn he'd run off with Madame Lescalopier, but no, she's confined to bed with a sore throat. She doesn't know him at all."

She sat staring, lost in thought, at the ginger, saffron and nutmegs.

"He said something very curious when he left," she continued after a while. "He said that God had summoned him. I didn't believe him at the time. Do you think it possible he was telling the truth?"

Monsieur Coquereau got up and threw a log on the fire.

"Why shouldn't it be the truth?" he said. "The fellow was a simpleton, and simpletons are the playthings of the great. Perhaps, like them, the Almighty was merely trifling with him."